EXTRAORDINARY THOUGHTS OF JONAH PALADIN

... an ancient story of challenges,

choices & consequences

Russell R. Esposito

Extraordinary Thoughts
of
Jonah Paladin
…an ancient story of challenges, choices & consequences

Copyright @ 2014 Russell R. Esposito

Published and printed in the United States of America by
The New York Learning Library www.tnyll.com

A Family Fables Book

Family Fables is an imprint of The New York Learning Library. All rights reserved.

International Standard Book Number:
Printed book ISBN 13: 9780967143620
(eBook ISBN 978-0-9671436-3-7)
ISBN: 0967143624

First Edition 2014

Cover Design - by Angie Zambrano

This book is dedicated to my family…

❖ *To my wife, for her love, intelligence, support and enriching insights.*

❖ *To my children, for their love and individually unique views and thoughts.*

❖ *To my father-in-law, for his constant kindness, enduring friendship, wisdom and good humor.*

❖ *And to my father, who taught the value and satisfaction gained from persistence, patience and hard work.*

CONTENTS

⇒⇇ ⇇⇒

GRANDPA'S DISCOVERY

I T WAS THE LAST DAY, the last day we would own the family farm in Liguria. I was still in high school the winter my grandfather sold it. He lived alone on the farm, but kept himself occupied by reading books. Actually, he did more than occasionally read books, the way most people do. Instead, my grandfather read every day, and often all day. He devoured countless books, as if books were an essential nutrient or somehow necessary for daily survival. It was rare indeed to see him without a book in his hands, or within easy reach of one.

Often my grandfather would become so intrigued by a book that he would ignore a ringing telephone, and neglect to check his mailbox for days at a time. Someone would drive over to check on him, and predictably find Grandpa with his head buried in a book, and barely looking up to see who walked into his house. It became customary to expect only a wave from his hand, and a muttered invitation to help yourself in the kitchen.

One time, I actually walked into his house, ate an entire shepherd's pie in the kitchen, and then loudly announced, "Goodbye Grandpa." But before I left, I peeked at him from behind a door. He never even flinched. Without lifting an eye off his book, my grandfather simply called out, "Later Jack." Well, at least he seemed to know that it was me in his kitchen. Although everyone in my family insists to this very day that it was just a lucky guess on his part.

As a result of his obsession with books, my grandfather knew a great deal about a variety of diverse subjects. And he had become well known for his ability to deliver an avalanche of information when explaining the finer points of a topic.

But my grandfather wasn't exclusively a serious minded fact-filled man, the kind who might be eternally focused on facts alone. No, my grandfather had another side, an entertaining and humorous side. When he wasn't reading, he was often telling a story, or sometimes even provoking a controversy among us grandkids. You know, just to stir up some excitement. Like the time he asked us, "What if someone uses a dog whistle that only dogs can hear, but no dogs are there to hear it, does the whistle make a sound?" That question incited a sizeable squabble among us grandkids. And our noisy debate quickly brought Grandpa's barking dog into the fray, who seemingly had an opinion to voice on this canine controversy as well. The scene quickly developed into a blasting uproar of yelling kids and a yelping dog.

And then there was the time we agreed to play an unusual dice game with my grandfather. When we finished, he had won almost all of our Halloween candy. We couldn't understand how Grandpa kept winning, until he explained that the special dice he used were "nontransitive." We had no idea what he was talking about, but we knew enough to bitterly complain that he cheated us by using the special dice in his game. Of course, Grandpa returned our sugary bounty along with a lecture on the dangers and pitfalls of gambling. But we also learned that we all very much wanted a set of "nontransitive dice" of our own.

My grandfather liked to describe the chaos that he sometimes triggered, as nothing more than "spirited educational debates." Without a doubt, he knew how to ignite controversy and conversation. But he was also a skilled and gifted storyteller, and that truly was his greater glory. He had an endless supply of stories and some were very funny. And yet, we were never completely certain if a story was true, or if Grandpa "improved upon the truth" a little, just to make his stories more amusing. Sometimes, we suspected that he added little details to his stories that he took from different books he had read. But whether his stories were completely true or not, no one really seemed to care. We just enjoyed listening, always expecting some improbable but funny twist to arise in the story.

Anyway, my chore on that last day seemed pretty easy. All I had to do was get to the farm by taxi, and help my grandfather load boxes of his favorite books into the taxi's trunk, along with a few other personal items. And then take a short ride to my uncle's house, where my grandfather would soon call his home.

But somehow, whenever Grandpa is involved, you should always expect the unexpected.

The taxi pulled up to the farm, the fields were brownish gray, frozen and empty, except for the wind that was always present in the winter season. When the taxi finally stopped in front of Grandpa's house, I jumped out into that wicked wind. If you had heard the sound of that wind ripping through the farm's wire fence, you'd swear it was the howl of some strange animal wailing in the wilderness. It was an awful sound that could put a chill in your back faster than the worst winter winds.

As I glanced at the trembling wire fence while walking up the porch steps there was a sudden… *CRASH!* The loud noise came from inside the house. Quickly, I pushed open the front door and rushed inside to see my grandfather sitting on the kitchen floor among lots of broken bits and pieces. It looked like broken ceramics, glass or something. And there was a hole, kind of an opening in the floor near him.

"Grandpa, are you ok?"

"Jack," exclaimed my grandfather, "come here."

"What happened? What crashed? Are you all right?" I asked again while looking around the room.

"Sit next to me," Grandpa replied. His hand brushed away some broken pieces to make room for me on the floor.

Grandpa seemed to be ok, so I sat down beside him.

"You won't believe what happened today Jack. I was going from room to room saying goodbye to this old place. You know, this house is the only home I've ever known. It's been in our family for many generations. Anyway, my final room was here, the kitchen."

My grandfather pushed his index finger on the kitchen floor while looking down at it. Then Grandpa laughed as he remembered one of his favorite kitchen stories.

Naturally, I should have seen this coming. We all cherished Grandpa's little stories and chats, but sometimes Grandpa took our conversations off track and onto detours of his choosing. So, my grandfather ignored the mess on the floor, as well as my question, and continued with his kitchen story.

"Jack, it was a few years ago, but do you remember the time we left our dog, Bruno, alone with a roast in the kitchen."

Patiently, I smiled and nodded.

Grandpa pointed to the kitchen table. "That big old hound jumped right onto that very table and was happily enjoying himself. At least, until he felt the whack of your grandmother's wooden spoon on his back." Grandpa chuckled while shaking his head. "Your grandmother scrambled around this kitchen chasing after that big dog while swinging her spoon in a wild frenzy, and breaking more things than he did!"

We both laughed.

"That wooden spoon was your grandmother's weapon-of-choice I always said. She would whirl it high over her head to deal with you grandkids too. In her hand that spoon sliced through the air like the baton of a hyperactive bandleader."

I chuckled. "Oh, we all remember Grandma's wooden spoon. She really knew how to get our attention with it."

Grandpa nodded and laughed. "She was a little woman but awfully feisty for her size."

"That's for sure Grandpa."

One of his eyebrows rose, and he looked over at me. I smiled as we both remembered Grandma's high-energy antics... before she became ill and finally passed on.

A moment passed.

Then I picked up a few pieces of the shattered jumble scattered around us, and took a closer look at these broken bits of something.

I held them up for my grandfather to see.

"So Grandpa, what is this stuff? What happened here, and why is there a hole in the floor?"

"Jack, let me tell you what happened. When I walked over to sit at the kitchen table and wait for you, I stepped on a squeaky floorboard. The board always squeaked, but today it seemed just a little bit louder. It's probably just my imagination. Anyway, I lifted my foot and stepped down again. *Squeak*. And again... *Squeak*... like it was trying to get my attention. Then I looked down at the board and noticed that a corner was slightly raised. To get a better look, I sat down on the floor and felt along the length of the board. It was a little warped and loose too, it's no wonder it squeaked all these years. Just being curious, I used my pocketknife to pry up the raised corner, and the board easily lifted up and out. To my surprise, I saw there was something down there under the floor. As I looked more closely, I realized it was a round ceramic jar. I pushed away some cobwebs, lifted it out and wiped off the dust. The jar was tan with blue stripes and had two handles."

"A jar? How did it get down there?"

My grandfather shrugged his shoulders. "I haven't a clue how it got there. But I can tell you that it looked like an old amphora jar, the kind used many years ago for storing and preserving food, usually fruit... at least until it was smashed to smithereens." He pointed to the broken mess around us on the floor.

"Smashed? How or by who? Is anyone else in the house?" I asked while looking around. Grandpa never paid much attention to who came in, especially when he was reading an interesting book.

"Jack, no one is here but us. And I did it. I smashed it."

"You mean you dropped it?"

"No, I *smashed* it. Just like a piñata," he joked. "Except I didn't have a stick to swing at it, so I did this." Grandpa swiftly swung his arms down to show how he smashed it against the floor.

"You smashed it? Like a piñata?"

Grandpa nodded, but was unable to hide his grin. He looked a bit like a little kid who delighted in doing something he knew he shouldn't have done.

"But why Grandpa?"

"Jack, I had no choice, the jar's cover was sealed with wax."

I shook my head. "But Grandpa, why not scrape off the wax, or somehow pry off the lid to see what's inside? Why smash the whole jar?"

Grandpa smiled. "I agree Jack, so let me explain. I lit a candle and used it to melt away the wax, and the lid easily fell off the jar. When I looked inside, I faintly saw something, but it didn't look like any kind of food. Then I reached into the jar, and I was astonished to find a book in there. This book!"

My grandfather raised his hand to show me. It was a small brown leather-bound book.

"And Jack, I know what you are thinking. You're curious about the book, but still wondering why I smashed the jar after I got the lid off."

"Right." I nodded and smiled.

"Well, there was a problem Jack. The book was too large to fit through the mouth of the open jar. It was like a model ship stuck in a bottle. There was no way to get the book out. Except… you know… *crash*. So, the jar became a flying piñata, as I smashed it down onto the floor. And the book fell out, perfectly preserved."

"Well, ok Grandpa, at least now I know what happened here." I laughed. "But a flying piñata? This qualifies as *flying*?" I swung my arms down toward the floor as he had demonstrated just moments ago.

"Sure Jack. That's flying." Grandpa grinned. "It was a short flight… crash landed... no casualties… and all pages survived."

I nodded and chuckled, "Ok, if you say so Grandpa."

Then Grandpa held out the book for me to take.

In my hands, I carefully looked over the book, but couldn't find any printing on the front or back covers.

My grandfather said, "Go ahead. Open it. Just be careful the pages are old and a little fragile."

Gently, I opened the old book. Centered on the first page were these strange words.

FABULA SCRIBO
ANNUM 1494

My grandfather pointed to the words and explained. "The words *Fabula Scribo* are Latin meaning *Story Written*, and *Annum 1494* means *Year 1494*." He continued, "So this tells us that we've discovered a story that was written over 500 years ago! And this book has been hidden under our kitchen floorboards for at least a few generations."

With this mysterious old book in my hands, I slowly turned to the next page. Now gazing at the faded text on the old paper, I read the book's title, and the first chapter's heading out loud.

"EXTRAORDINARY
THOUGHTS
OF
JONAH PALADIN"

CHAPTER 1
HORROR IN THE MONK'S
NEST... THEN A CONTEST

I looked up from the page at my grandfather and asked, "Have you ever heard of Jonah Paladin? And what's a monk?"

"Never heard of him, the book is a mystery to me too. But Jack, I can tell you something about monks."

Wondering how much detail he would offer, I looked at Grandpa hoping for a quick explanation.

"Jack, a monk is kind of like a priest that lives in a monastery far from towns and most people." Grandpa explained, "Centuries ago, many monks were scholars and researched different subjects for the Church. They lived mostly solitary lives with other monks researching scientific or historical topics, and translating ancient books into Latin. Some monks were astronomers dedicated to mysteries like finding the true date of Easter. Also, a Benedictine monk invented musical notation in the 11th century, and of course..."

My grandfather had to be stopped! Grandpa is a wealth of information, and can easily discuss almost any subject for hours. Evidently, he knows a lot about famous monks too. Pretty amazing. And clearly, he was ready to tell me much more than I wanted to know.

"Grandpa, please," I interrupted. "Ok, I know enough about monks now, so let's get back to the book. I'm still confused. What's a monk doing in a *nest*?"

Grandpa looked just a little annoyed at me for stopping him, but then shook his head. "Jack, I don't know either. We'll have to read on to find out. Let's sit in the living room. The furniture is still there, it won't be moved out until tomorrow."

So, we got up off the floor and made ourselves comfortable on the large sofa-chairs. By this time the taxi driver, Charlie, an old friend of Grandpa's had come inside and joined us as well. It seemed Charlie was looking for any excuse to get out of his taxi, and enjoyed settling down in a large soft chair. Grandpa eased himself into another comfortable chair between us, and opened the book.

And so, that last day of the family farm was the first day we read this ancient story. It's a story about the astonishing adventures of Jonah Paladin, and a girl named Julia he met during his challenging odyssey. Grandpa and I took turns reading until we finished the entire book. And we learned that this old book is truly about... *challenges, choices & consequences.*

CHAPTER 1

HORROR IN THE MONK'S NEST... THEN A CONTEST

A long, long time ago, someone was sleeping deep in the forest of ancient Liguria...

IT WAS EARLY MORNING, and the damp air was quiet and still. Then from nowhere, there was the sound of a thud. The monk's peaceful slumber was now broken by a curious noise... *THUD, THUD, THUD.* He stayed under his sheepskin bedcovers trying to figure out what was making the unusual sound. Then it stopped, but the monk waited several minutes before deciding to get up.

The simple brown robes worn by the monk straightened as he finally stood up in the hollow of his nest... a nest that he built from branches, leaves and sheepskins at the highest crown of a huge elm tree. As he stretched legs and arms, his tall and slender frame fully appeared. He looked down from his treetop perch. Searching with a steady gaze, the monk scanned below trying to find out what was making this strange sound.

The sound the monk heard was unfamiliar and troubling. As the monk looked down from his nest, his eyes quickly riveted onto something... something terrifying. It was an archer, mostly concealed in the shadows and standing with bow drawn and arrow at the ready. And aimed right at him! In the next instant, the monk saw the point of an arrowhead in front of his face. In a flash of fear, he swiftly ducked down as the arrow flew by, scarcely above his head.

Now with his head down low in the nest and face pressed against thick sheepskins, the monk heard another *THUD*. Immediately he realized, *My God, that's what made the sounds that woke me. Arrows!* More arrows struck the nest... *THUD, THUD*. The monk looked horrified. He worried, *Could an arrow penetrate the nest's wall?* Arrows continued to hit the nest. Then instantly, he felt a burning in his leg. He reached down and felt a warm liquid. He glanced at his hand... *blood!* An arrow had found its way though the nest's structure and struck his leg. Wincing in pain the monk pulled the arrow out of his thigh with one hard tug. Blood was running out of his wound. Working rapidly, he tore a strip of cloth from his robe and tied it around his leg to slow the bleeding. But soon the cloth was red, drenched with blood. As the monk started to tie another strip of cloth over it, he heard... *THUD, THUD.*

Hopelessly trapped, the monk's mind raced, and his leg ached badly. There was no escape from the deadly arrows. His thoughts were a swirling tempest of terror. He began to sweat. There was nothing the monk could do... *but pray.*

For the last year, the monk had spent many days deep in the forest, up high in his treetop nest. But he did not *hike* through the forest to reach his nest. He *climbed* through the forest. And he did not simply climb up trees... he climbed *across* them.

He traveled high above the ground through this dense old forest climbing across the treetops, reaching out from branch to branch. The trees in this ancient forest were very close to each other, and branches touched creating kind of a wooden web. The monk climbed through this forest's web until he reached his nest, which was positioned at the forest's edge overlooking a vineyard.

But this vineyard was special. It was actually a large maze. Its vine-covered fencing was carefully arranged with many turns leading to dead ends. And the maze was as twisted as the grapevines from which it was made. It was like a large puzzle meant to baffle and bewilder anyone who might enter. At its center was something just as odd as the maze itself… a small, round, windowless house. Often the monk looked down from his nest and watched the vineyard and house for hours at a time.

There was someone who lived alone in this round house that interested the monk. This someone was a mysterious, large man that was part creature, as his body was mostly covered with small feathers. Some called him a feathered giant, although he was not larger than the largest of men.

The monk often came to watch this feathered giant perform his daily chores. He closely watched the giant working in the vineyard, and studied his every move. The monk carefully observed how the giant performed his tasks, what he ate, and when he slept. The monk wanted to know every detail about the giant, and so he spent many quiet days up high in his nest, just watching and learning about this mysterious manlike creature.

But this day was different, very different… it was anything but quiet. The monk's nest was under attack! Arrows struck the nest and then the monk's leg.

As the monk tightened the bandage wrapped around his bloody leg, he wondered if this would be his last day in the nest… and perhaps his last day on earth. But the monk was comforted by the fact that he was very high up in a tall tree. He reasoned that if this was to be his last day on earth, at least his soul could more easily travel up to the heavens to meet his Creator.

Meanwhile, in the distance, on the other side of this ancient forest, there was a charming town with a castle. The castle was small, but so dazzling and beautiful that everyone called it the town's "jewel-box." Near the castle was a splendid stable with horses of different breeds from around the world. Some were exotic horses from such far away places as Arabia, Persia, and Catai in the Far East. The horses were magnificent animals and very well trained. But there so happened to be one horse that was different than other horses. This horse was wild. So wild that no one could ride and tame him, not even the skilled stable master.

One day, the town's King Leo proposed a contest for the people's amusement. He offered a prize of gold coins to anyone who could ride this wild stallion that would kick and buck off whoever tried to mount. And so, a date was set for this contest, and all were invited to try their best.

CHAPTER 2

A SOLUTION IN THE SHADOWS

ON THE DAY of the King's contest many skilled riders arrived well prepared to compete for the prize. But one-by-one each rider was promptly thrown from this horribly wild horse. Of course, not all the riders who came were skillful. Some were clumsy riders, and others were absolutely awful and couldn't even mount the beast. These unskilled lads found themselves chasing after this wild horse that seemed to enjoy the spectacle, lightly prancing away from these riders with no chance of catching up.

So foolish were these fellows that they might very well have had bunches of broccoli bundled inside their leathery heads where brains ought to have been. Nonetheless, the pure comedy of it added to the crowd's amusement. People roared with laughter while these broccoli-brained buffoons haplessly ran around. Some of these unfortunate fellows insisted they were paid by the King to amuse the crowd by acting daffy and witless. These dubious claims caused still more laughter among the spectators, some screeched and fell over laughing hysterically. It has long been said that comedy springs from tragedy, so long as it's another's tragedy. And that surely was the case on this day.

Watching the entire contest was a young lad named Jonah Paladin. Jonah had a longish mop of hair, wore patched clothing, and looked as poor as a country church mouse. He watched every rider with keen interest, and especially the more skillful riders. Jonah watched each rider mount, and studied the horse's furious reactions. He observed every movement of the horse, and noted how and when it shook its head and torso. Jonah watched each brief but turbulent ride, and no one was successful. Each rider was thrown from this beast of a horse that day.

When the contest was over with no winner, Jonah thought to himself, *If only I had a chance, I could ride and tame that wild horse.* Jonah was a very optimistic and cheerful lad. His spirit and nature would not allow him to easily harbor a negative thought.

Several years ago, when Jonah was a little boy, his friend was surprised to find lumps of dry horse dung in his Christmas stocking. It was put in there by the boy's parents to teach him a lesson, since his behavior at times was awful that year.

Young Jonah said to his friend, "You have a stocking full of horse dung? Maybe that means your parents got you a horse for Christmas. Let's check out back!"

For the better or worse, Jonah only saw the joy and good in things. So, of course this high-spirited lad could watch expert riders be thrown from a wild stallion, yet would still think he could ride the animal and win the contest. But Jonah wasn't simply watching the contest, he was also thinking carefully and had figured out a plan for riding this wild horse. He rushed home to tell his parents about the contest and his plan.

Still breathing fast from running home, Jonah rushed up to his father and quickly blurted out, "Papa, I think I know how to ride that wild horse and win the King's contest."

Jonah's father, busy with candle making, looked up from his work. "Now Jonah, slow down. What are you saying about the King's contest?"

Jonah was almost too excited to speak. He took a deep breath. "I'm saying, I can ride the King's wild horse and win the contest and reward."

Looking a little worried, his father stopped working and put down the candle tallow and casts. "Hold on now, Jonah, how did this idea get into your head? That horse is a wild one from what I've heard. You would probably get hurt trying to ride him."

Looking straight into his father's eyes, Jonah stepped closer. "I think I know why the horse kicks and bucks every rider, and so, I have a plan."

"Oh, you have a plan?" His father looked skeptical and scratched his chin.

"Yes." Jonah winked confidently.

"Alright, I'm listening," his father said patiently.

Jonah continued, "I'm almost sure about this. I think the horse is afraid of his own shadow."

His father listened as Jonah described how and when each rider got into trouble with the horse.

Jonah explained, "Each time a rider was thrown from the horse, the sun was behind the horse casting a shadow."

His father nodded, but looked unconvinced. "Well, maybe the horse did see his shadow each time, but we don't know that's *why* he bucked. And even if you're right, how would you keep the horse from seeing his own shadow? You can't block the sun."

"No, I can't block the sun." Jonah paused. "But a mountain can."

His father focused trying to understand.

"My idea is to ride just after the sun sets behind the Mountains of Liguria. At dusk there is still some light, but not enough to create shadows."

His father looked concerned. "Well Jonah, it may be true that there are no shadows at dusk, but the horse may still give you lots of trouble. Jonah, you're young and still an inexperienced rider. That horse could hurt you. The contest's prize money is not as important as your safety."

Listening from another room, Jonah's mother approached and agreed. "Jonah please, just forget about the contest. You're too young for that kind of horse. Anyway, I never heard of a horse being afraid of his own shadow."

Over the next few days, Jonah followed his parents around the house pestering them about the horse at every opportunity. Jonah kept asking to ride, and insisting he was old enough to try. One time, his father stepped backwards not knowing Jonah was standing silently behind him. Tripping over Jonah, his father stumbled but managed to regain his balance.

"Jonah, can you give me a little space? The last few days you've circled me like a dog on the hunt."

Jonah's mother added, "All you do is linger nearby and talk about the contest and that horse. That's all we hear about. It's like there's an echo in here. But unlike a real echo, your voice Jonah never fades away and stops."

Jonah frowned and lowered his gaze, as he listened to his parents' grumblings.

But now his mother was feeling a little badly about her last echo comment, and decided to lighten the mood by telling an old story about a little girl and her echo.

"Actually Jonah, all this talk reminds me of a story about a caretaker who raised his little girl in a monastery where he worked and lived. Each December the girl would go to the top of the monastery's tall tower and shout out her Christmas list. She hoped that Saint Nicholas would hear her echoing voice over and over as it bounced among the mountaintops." His mother smiled. "The girl's voice was heard for miles around, but I'm not so sure her list ever reached the ears of Saint Nicholas. I've heard that it's a true story. Clever little girl."

And as his mother had hoped, the little story did help, and a smile began to return to Jonah's face. But Jonah's mother didn't know that telling this little story to Jonah would one day be of great importance.

CHAPTER 3

ASK THE RIGHT QUESTION
THE RIGHT WAY

SEVERAL DAYS HAD PASSED and Jonah had not mentioned the contest or the horse even once. But Jonah wasn't one to give up easily, and still believed his plan would work. He began to think if he could only convince his father, then his mother might also go along with the idea. So, Jonah began asking his father again about the contest. And after pestering his poor father a few more times, his father did what most parents do with harassing, nagging teenagers… he gave up!

Reluctantly, his father said, "Jonah, riding that horse will be like trying to hold a cat by its tail... a punishing experience. I wouldn't want any part of that horse or the cat's tail either. I think you're too young for this horse and contest. But if you're so sure of your plan, then go and ask the King's stable master, Malvagio, if he will let you ride this wild stallion."

"Really?" Jonah grinned. He couldn't believe his ears.

"Yes, but tell Malvagio your age, and ask him if you are too young to ride the horse."

"Thank you Papa, but... ummm... I might ask him just a little bit differently."

"Ask him just a little bit differently? What do you mean Jonah?"

"Papa, I will tell him my age, but maybe I'll ask if I'm *old enough* to ride, instead of asking if I'm *too young* to ride," Jonah said smiling.

"Ok, I get it Jonah, you want to plant the words *old enough* into Malvagio's head. So, go ahead and ask him the way you want. Asking your way might just get the 'yes' answer you want."

His father thought about the subtle wording difference that his son cleverly suggested, chuckled and added, "Well, I'm not certain that you're *old enough* to ride, but you're certainly *smart enough*. Jonah, just promise to be careful. When... sorry... I mean *if* you're thrown from this horse, stay clear of his kicking legs, and get to the fence as fast as you can."

Jonah hugged his father. "Thanks again Papa, I'll be careful."

"Ok Jonah, go ask Malvagio now, and I'll tell your mother after you're gone. She won't like this at all." Looking a bit worried he mumbled, "I'll have to beg for forgiveness instead of ask for permission."

Jonah went to visit Malvagio at the King's stable and asked if he was old enough to enter the contest and ride the horse. Malvagio thought for only a moment, then agreed it was ok for Jonah to ride. He reasoned Jonah's ride would provide another day of entertainment for the townsfolk, and scheduled a date for the contest. And the contest time was set for dusk, as Jonah requested, when the sun sets behind the mountains to the west.

CHAPTER 4
ASK A DIFFERENT QUESTION,
GET A DIFFERENT ANSWER

MEANWHILE, Jonah's father, Dan, approached his wife, Madaline, to let her know that Jonah was on his way to ask about entering the King's contest. Dan sat on the couch beside her. He had a strategy for breaking the news to her.

"Madaline, do you remember that funny story your cousin Phil tells when he thought he wanted to become a priest, and went to study in the monastery?"

"Not sure, Dan, which story do you mean? That was so many years ago."

"Well, your cousin Phil," Dan laughed a little, "told us that he and a friend at the monastery would get bored praying at the grotto. And one day his friend suggested they play cards while praying there. So, your cousin went to his priest and asked if he could play cards while praying, and of course the priest told him no. That story, Madaline, do you remember it?" Dan asked as he chuckled.

"Oh yes, I remember," Madaline laughed. "And the next day my cousin Phil went to the grotto and his friend, Vince, had a shuffled deck of playing cards and was ready to deal a game. Phil was surprised and told Vince that he had already asked the priest if they could play cards while praying and was told no. But Vince said that he also asked the priest, and was told it was ok."

Dan laughed a little louder in anticipation. "Madaline, do you remember the rest the story?"

"Sure, no one could forget this one! My cousin asked his friend Vince, how could the priest have given him a different answer? And Vince explained that he asked the priest a different question. Vince didn't ask if it was ok to *play cards while praying*, but instead asked the priest if it was ok to *pray while playing cards*. And of course the priest said, yes, you can pray anywhere and anytime, regardless of whether you're peeling carrots or playing cards!"

Dan and Madaline both laughed.

"Dan, those two boys really where rascals. It's no wonder neither were allowed to finish up and become priests."

"Probably a good thing," Dan chuckled.

"Agree." Madaline nodded.

"But Dan, why are you bringing up that old story now?"

Dan cleared his throat. "Our son, Jonah, just said something that reminded me of how Vince asked the priest just a little bit differently to get the 'yes' answer he wanted."

"Really? What did Jonah say to you?"

"Well, you see, he's been bugging me again about the King's contest, and insisting he's old enough to ride that horse. Jonah is growing up fast, and you do know how really smart he is."

"Growing up fast?" Madaline huffed. "Dan, please don't tell me you agreed he's old enough to ride?"

"Madaline, please just listen to what happened…"

CHAPTER 5

MALVAGIO THE SHREWD STABLE MASTER

THE DAY FOR JONAH TO RIDE this wild horse finally arrived. And the evening sky offered a most magnificent sunset. A crowd gathered and watched the sun go down behind the local mountains, as everyone waited to watch Jonah ride. People there talked about everyday matters. Among them was a salty old sailor who commented to his friend, "Red sky at night, a sailor's delight," which means tonight's red sunset would bring beautiful weather tomorrow morning.

Finally, looking a little nervous, Jonah approached the horse but easily mounted. He gave a slight kick with his worn boots, and the horse began to calmly trot. The amazed crowd was silent as everyone watched closely. The horse gave Jonah no sign of trouble. He rode slowly as he reached the far end of the corral, then carefully turned around and easily rode back to where he had started.

The crowd roared with cheers, and hats were tossed up into the air.

The ecstatic King Leo stood and shouted, "Bravo, Jonah Paladin!" He promptly handed a bag of gold coins to this astonishing lad who could ride this terrible horse.

Jonah rushed home and threw open the door. Confident and victorious, he waved the bag of coins high above his head. His parents were thrilled to see him so happy, and also relieved that he wasn't injured. Now with both hands raised up in the air and a victorious smile, Jonah joyfully joked, "And now where's that cat's tail we talked about?"

Feeling generous the next day, King Leo told the stable master, "No one, not even you Malvagio, can ride this horse. Let's give the horse to that youth Jonah. Yesterday, he rode without even a hint of trouble. He was incredible."

Malvagio, a proud old stable master, was jealous of Jonah's successful ride, and did not want to give away the horse. *That lad just had a lucky ride,* he thought to himself, *I am the only maestro of this stable and that horse. This embarrassment must stop.*

And so, clever Malvagio quickly suggested to the King that another challenge be proposed to the lad as a way to win the horse.

"Dear King, instead of giving away the horse now, may I suggest that we challenge this young fellow to ride three times to win the horse." He told the King, "Jonah has completed one ride already, if he can succeed with two additional rides, he would win the horse. And throughout our fair town, these two additional rides will build much anticipation and prolong the amusement for everyone!"

The King liked the idea, and so the challenge was offered to Jonah who happily accepted this chance to win the horse. And again Jonah's request to ride at dusk was granted.

The day of Jonah's second ride came at last. And predictably, the evening sunset was right on time. The clocks of our universe keep perfect time, ever since the Creator first wound them up.

Once more, the evening's sunset was spectacular, inspiring the same old sailor to again recite the adage, "Red sky at night, a sailor's delight."

Malvagio, hearing the old sailor's comment for the second time, began to think... *sunset again... hmmm...*

maybe the dim light of dusk is just the right time to ride this wild horse. Perhaps Jonah may not be able to ride during the bright light of day.

Jonah entered the corral.

Malvagio watched as Jonah mounted the horse and went on to successfully complete his second ride without the slightest difficulty. The crowd cheered and roared once again at Jonah's easy triumph. Malvagio was now convinced that the dim light after sunset was the secret to Jonah's success, and shrewdly developed a plan to foil the lad's third ride.

So the next day, the old stable master suggested to the King that the crowd would be much larger if the third and final ride were to take place on Sunday morning after sunrise, and just before everyone in the town attends church.

The King listened and agreed, and so Malvagio set the date for Jonah's final ride to be next Sunday morning.

When Jonah learned the day and time set for his last ride, he was very surprised and alarmed. He raced into town to ask Malvagio why his final ride is scheduled for Sunday morning.

"But why, Malvagio? Why am I scheduled to ride Sunday morning? Why can't I ride at dusk, after the sun sets, as I did twice already?"

Old Malvagio simply replied, "The King has chosen Sunday morning just before the townsfolk attend church," and walked away without any further explanation.

On Saturday night before Jonah's final ride, Malvagio brought the finest carrots, oats and barley to the horse. "Here you go boy, eat up, we want you to have your full strength Sunday morning. When you buck Jonah make sure he's flung up high, and lands atop the tallest castle chimney! Oh, that would be just what he deserves. Ashes!" Malvagio shook his arms around and laughed as he imagined Jonah's bottom stuck in the chimney's opening with his arms and legs wildly flailing about.

CHAPTER 6

HELP FROM A PRIEST WITH A CAT

I T WAS EARLY SUNDAY MORNING and the time for Jonah's final ride was near. The sun had risen to a brilliantly clear sky.

Father Robert Croce, pastor of the town's church, St. John the Apostle, was already inside the church, and slowly walked to the back corner of the building. The elderly priest had a bowl of leftover fried fish in one hand, and his Sunday sermon in his other. When he stopped behind the last pew to place the bowl of cold fish on the floor, Caesar, his cat instantly appeared from beneath the priest's long robes and quickly started feasting. The poor little cat was blind in one eye and often walked along between Father Croce's shoes, under his robes, unknown to all others. Having vision in only one eye, the cat felt safe and enjoyed the protection of being under the priest's robes, where he often silently traveled. Caesar followed the old priest almost everywhere, sometimes even into the confessional booth, where the cat quietly rested while hearing whispers of the world's worries.

As Father Croce stood watching Caesar eat, he recited a particular verse from the Bible. With a smile on his face he said to the cat, "Render unto Caesar the things which are Caesar's, and unto God the things that are God's." This was Father Croce's little joke that he liked to share with Caesar every Sunday morning. The priest then walked up the staircase to the choir's balcony, where he would then *render unto God*, as he quietly practiced reading his Sunday morning sermon.

But this Sunday morning something happened. Father Croce heard someone enter the church, but it was early and the Sunday services would not begin for some time. He looked up from his reading and listened to a voice coming from a back pew beneath the balcony. Curiously, it sounded like someone was praying for clouds.

As the priest peeked down from the balcony, he wondered why anyone would pray for clouds? Father Croce saw a young man looking skyward saying,

"Clouds, I need thick clouds. But looking at the light coming through the stained glass windows, I can tell the sun is still shinning brightly outside."

Father Croce walked down the balcony steps and over to Jonah, who he recognized, and sat next to him.

"Good morning. You're Jonah Paladin, right? You rode the King's wild horse, am I right?"

Jonah replied, "Yes, Father Croce, good morning."

"Jonah, I apologize, but I overheard your prayer. And if I heard you correctly, you're praying for clouds, which is a bit unusual. And I don't expect you'll see any today. The sky is bright, and as blue as a patch of pale periwinkles."

Jonah looked down and nodded in agreement.

"But why do you want clouds Jonah?"

Jonah looked up at the priest. "Father, can I tell you a secret?"

Father Croce smiled and nodded gently.

Jonah continued, "I'm almost certain that the horse I rode is frightened by his own shadow. I'll be riding the horse again this morning, and a cloudy sky would prevent shadows and keep the horse from being frightened."

Father Croce listened carefully, his eyes squinting a little while focusing on Jonah words.

Jonah explained further, "My past two rides were at dusk, right after sunset. At dusk the light is too dim to produce shadows, and so the horse wasn't frightened and didn't buck or kick."

Jonah paused.

The priest quietly stared at him.

"So, Father, I need clouds to block the bright sunlight and prevent shadows. I can't ride today without clouds. It's impossible."

Father Croce thought for a moment. He rubbed his gray beard. "Really? But in any case, you already rode this horse twice. Is that right?"

"Yes," answered Jonah.

"So Jonah, I have a thought on this, may I share it with you?"

Jonah's eyebrow rose. "Sure."

"Jonah, I think that you're letting fear control your destiny. So many great ideas are lost because people fear failure. Too often we yield to fear, and invent excuses and reasons for not doing something. Too often we tell ourselves.... if only I had the time... or if only I were younger." The priest paused, then added, "or if only I had clouds."

The priest smiled at Jonah, who was quietly listening.

"Jonah, you're focusing on reasons *not* to ride, instead of the reasons why you *should* ride. Don't focus on the negative. Negatives lead nowhere. Focus on positives. You successfully rode this horse twice already. Focus on those successes. Look Jonah, the horse knows you now, he already let you ride him twice. This is a different horse, and a new day. Don't lose sight of the new situation, and a new opportunity. A new day does not require the old way. Let go of the old way. You have to think a little differently now. You don't need clouds anymore Jonah."

Father Croce hesitated then said, "But you will need something else."

"What?" Jonah softly questioned.

"Fiducia," answered the priest.

"Fiducia?" asked Jonah looking puzzled.

"It's the Latin word for confidence and trust. All you need now is confidence. Trust in yourself." Leaning closer he said, "Jonah, you need the same courage and confidence you had the first time you mounted this wild horse at dusk. And show no fear. For if you do, the horse will sense it and buck you right off. Also, before you mount him, let him see you, then stroke the side of his head. And talk to him, so he hears a familiar voice. And when you turn your back toward the sun and shadows appear before you, sit tight in the saddle and ride with confidence. And stroke your horse's head again while firmly telling him to settle down. Trust me. This horse already knows you, and he will let you ride again regardless of any shadows that might appear."

"Thanks for the advice, Father, but I'm not so sure that confidence is all I'll need. Confidence *and* clouds would be much better," replied Jonah.

Father Croce persisted. "Jonah, confidence is one of the most important things in life. Believe in yourself. Have faith. Then everything else falls into place. Jonah, you have nothing to lose, and a horse to gain. Just be confident and I'm sure that's all you'll need to succeed today."

Jonah thought for a few moments. He knew that he needed to decide very soon. The time for his ride was approaching.

Then Jonah's head nodded quickly. "Ok, I need to do this. You're right. I did ride successfully twice already. I need to be more confident, and focus on the positives. And with or without clouds, after getting this far, I have to ride this one last time. Thank you very much for the great advice, Father, and for your vote of confidence too. You've been a very big help to me."

Jonah stood, and shook Father Croce's hand.

"Good luck Jonah, I know you'll be fine," Father Croce reassured him again.

Jonah waved goodbye, as he left through the church's large front doors.

Father Croce walked back to the balcony staircase. But before he could take his first step up, Caesar ran out from between his shoes, almost tripping the elderly priest. The cat ran up the steps ahead of the pastor, always wanting to stay close to his gentle master.

CHAPTER 7
THE IMPORTANCE OF BEING CONFIDENT

A ND SO, JONAH LEFT THE CHURCH and headed for the stable hoping for the best. Father Croce would soon follow, wanting to watch Jonah ride again, and praying his advice would help Jonah succeed.

As Jonah walked through the town on his way to the stable, many people leaned out of windows and stood on balconies to wish Jonah good luck. They waved flags, pillowcases, and scarves shouting, "Good luck Jonah," and "Hope you win the horse." People on the street clapped as Jonah passed by, wishing him well, and many walked along with him to the stable.

At the stable Jonah saw a large and growing crowd dressed in their Sunday best gathering for the contest. Jonah was nervous as he entered the corral. *The die is cast. There's no turning back now*, he thought to himself.

Jonah carefully walked over to the horse, and took hold of the bridle. He looked the horse in the eyes, and stroked the animal's head while saying, "Now behave my friend. Behave."

Then Jonah turned the horse a bit to face the sun and avoid any shadows. He mounted and stroked the horse's head a few more times, "Steady boy, good boy." Jonah thought, *This is the easy part. No shadows yet.* He gave a slight kick, and the horse started to trot. Jonah easily rode to the far end of the corral where they stopped. Slowly they tuned and the sun was now behind them. Suddenly, shadows appeared on the ground and the horse began to rear up on his hind legs! Jonah braced himself expecting the worst, but thought, *I might fall off this beast, but at least my theory about the shadows was right.*

Malvagio watched, and a little grin began to slowly spread across the cracked skin of his old weathered face. He thought, *My plan worked. Jonah can't ride this horse in the bright daylight. Now come on you beast, buck Jonah high up into the air!*

Jonah held his legs tightly around the horse. He leaned forward, and stroked the bucking horse while firmly saying, "Easy you, eeeeasy now." The horse bucked again with more ferocity, and poor Jonah thought he would soon be thrown off. The horse kept kicking, but Jonah managed to hold on with one hand, and with his other hand stroke the horse's neck, while pleading, "Down boy, down." Finally, after a few more kicks, the horse stopped bucking, steadied, and Jonah was riding in control again.

A few spectators in the silent crowd started to slowly clap, as they began to believe that Jonah would soon finish his ride successfully.

Father Croce smiled inwardly, looked up at the sky and nodded slightly as if to say thank you.

Malvagio was speechless. He stared in disbelief. It seemed all his plans were about to meet with total failure.

Jonah and the horse then quietly trotted full circle in the corral, and finally stopped right where they had begun.

The crowd exploded with noise, as everyone cheered wildly!

The King happily gave away the horse to the brave lad.

After the celebration subsided, Jonah rode his new horse to the town's church, and for a brief moment stopped out front thankful for the priest's help. As Jonah left the church and headed home, he realized that although he did not get the clouds he wanted, he did get help but in a different way. And as he rode, Jonah could hear the church bells ringing behind him. The bells of St. John's were brighter and louder than all other Sundays. Father Croce pulled the rope on the steeple bells much harder that day. And the old priest pulled the steeple rope so hard that Caesar, who hung on the rope each Sunday to enjoy a little ride, fell off and swiftly scrambled back under the priest's robes for shelter.

At home, Jonah's proud parents told him to use the horse to travel to the Studium Generale collegium on the coast, and knew the gold coins could easily pay for the school's tuition.

"Get a good education," his father advised.

"You have a great opportunity," agreed his mother.

CHAPTER 8
THE KING'S FAILING HEALTH

THE YOUTHFUL JONAH left for two years of study, but traveled back to his home each Christmas, Easter and summer to visit his parents. When he finally graduated and returned home, he burst through the front door, and was immediately embraced by his parents who missed having him around. After they chatted for some time, Jonah's parents asked about his studies during this last year, always curious to learn more from Jonah about his experiences away. Jonah explained that among other subjects, he had studied foreign languages, geometry, architecture, and learned how to read music and practiced the violin.

Jonah said good day in Italian, "Bon Giorno." He continued in French, "Bon Jour," then in Spanish, "Buenos Dias," and finally in German, "Gutten Tag."

His parents beamed with satisfaction.

Jonah then explained the basic foundations of architecture, from Euclid's geometry to engineering designs by Vitruvius.

His father looked astonished. "Jonah, how in the world do you remember all these names, ideas and formulas?"

"Well, to help me study, I sometimes recited my math studies and formulas to a scarecrow behind the school."

Jonah jokingly added, "He never seemed to get tired of listening, regardless of how many times I recited my lessons." Looking at his parents, Jonah chuckled, "As you both know all too well, I can be like a persistent echo at times."

Jonah's parents laughed, and his mother replied, "Yes, and we dearly missed your echoes when you were away Jonah."

Jonah smiled. "And I missed you both too, it's great to be home."

Then after some time and further conversation, Jonah's father stopped talking and seemed a little troubled about something, as his face showed a more serious expression. He leaned a little closer to Jonah, and began to explain some unfortunate news about their King Leo, who had been so generous to them.

"Jonah, it breaks my heart to tell you that our kind King Leo has been sick for the last year, and no doctor knows how to reverse his failing health."

Hearing the news, the sadness in Jonah's eyes was obvious. King Leo was a wise and benevolent leader, and cherished by everyone for his intelligence and kindness.

They talked further after dinner, and their conversation turned to happier things. They enjoyed time together, hours flew by quickly until it was late, and then all retired to their bedrooms.

But as they slept, Jonah and his parents were unaware that a doctor had learned a secret that might save the King, and that a messenger sent by the King would soon visit their humble home.

CHAPTER 9

A CLUE FOUND IN A SORCERER'S RHYME

A T THE "JEWEL-BOX" CASTLE, the King's most loyal servant, Stanley, quietly approached the sick King's bedside.

"Pardon me King Leo."

"Hello, Stanley, how are you today? And Stanley, once again, please don't call me *King Leo* in private," answered the King weakly.

Stanley smiled. "Ok Leo, and I'm fine today, thanks for asking. And I have some good news for you."

"Good news?"

"I think so. Waiting in the hallway is a traveling doctor from beyond the mountains who believes he can help you. His name is Doctor Sano."

The King, though weary and weak, looked up and his gentle green eyes brightened just a bit. "Help me?"

"Yes, Leo, he says he can help you."

"How? Did he say?"

"He did explain. But I would like to let him in so he can speak with you directly."

"Of course, thank you Stanley please let him in."

Stanley opened the door, and the King's eyes quickly fixed onto a very odd looking man standing in his doorway. The doctor was short and round like a wine barrel, and had a head the size and shape of a large pumpkin. His ears stuck out like open carriage doors, and he had large hands with fingers as fat as sausages. The doctor's eyes, nose and mouth all seemed to be kind of squashed together as if the man had just sucked an entire bowl of lemons. And because of his tightly compressed face, it was difficult to see the doctor's little smile. Also, to say Dr. Sano's clothes were unfashionable would be very kind indeed. The doctor's weird clothing screamed with loud colors, and frankly the man looked rather bizarre. Dr. Sano's unusual appearance did not instill confidence or give hope to the King.

Nevertheless, the good King displayed no concern, smiled and politely offered, "Greetings Dr. Sano."

The doctor respectfully approached. "Good day Sire."

"Dr. Sano, please sit," as he pointed to a chair near his bedside.

"Thank you King Leo."

"So, Dr. Sano, I must tell you that I am feeling worse each day. Do you really know what this illness is?" King Leo asked in a low voice.

"Dear King, I can't give your illness a name or offer a medical diagnosis, but there may be a cure for this strange malady that afflicts you."

The King's eyes opened a bit wider. "I'm listening, you have my attention good doctor." The King tried to focus on the doctor's words, and not be distracted by the doctor's peculiar appearance and most odd attire.

"Sire, I believe what's needed is a feather from the feathered giant who lives past the forest."

In a slightly stronger voice, the King asked, "A feather? Really? What makes you think a feather from this creature would be of any benefit?"

"I can explain," the doctor pulled his chair closer. "King Leo, I was collecting medicinal plants at the edge of the forest when I saw a figure chopping down a tree. It was the sorcerer, Saggio, as you know he lives in a hut deep in the forest. As he chopped at this tree he spoke a strange rhyme, and landed a blow with his ax after each line was recited. Parts of the rhyme seem to make sense, but other parts are not intelligible, or perhaps are a riddle. Saggio repeated his rhyme several times as he chopped away, so I was able to write it down as I hid behind a large bush. May I read it to you?"

The King looked a bit baffled, but nodded.

Dr. Sano unfolded a piece of paper and recited the rhyme.

The giant's feather, the King will need,
To cure his sickness caused by greed. (chop)

A prince was turned to a feathery breed,
But can break the spell with just one good deed.
(chop)

Should this deed be done something happens to me,
But no one knows what that would be."
(final chop and tree falls)

Hearing the rhyme, King Leo moved to sit up in his bed. He spoke slowly and softly, as if to conserve his energy. "Hmmm... Saggio's rhyme is indeed partially a riddle that I don't fully understand either. But the sorcerer's first few sentences are clearly about my sickness. The sorcerer's predictions have been right before, so it is possible that this feather could help me. Nothing else has helped, I am desperate as you can see and willing to try this feather of course."

The doctor hesitated but then clarified. "Dear King, sadly, I am not in possession of a feather."

The King nodded with a blank stare. "Oh... I see... well then do you have any thoughts on how we might obtain a feather from the giant?" Looking discouraged, the King perceptively added, "Surely this will be a difficult challenge."

"Sire, I have the same concerns," answered the doctor. "And I have no ready answer. But I came to you today since I wanted you to know about the rhyme as soon as possible."

"Thank you Doctor Sano, I do appreciate your effort traveling here to meet with me."

The two silently thought for a while, and then talked over the problem, as they considered the danger involved with approaching the giant.

Then the King's face brightened. "What about that clever youth who rode the wildest horse in my stable. I think his name is Jonah... Jonah Paladin. He might be a great candidate for this challenge. I've heard that the lad has just returned home from two years of study. He's now a little more mature, older and wiser too."

Dr. Sano looked dubious. "But dear King, this task is a much greater challenge than breaking a wild horse," he cautioned.

"Yes," agreed King Leo, "but I recall hearing about someone who I think can help Jonah. I've been told there's a certain monk who spies on this giant from his treetop nest, and knows much about the giant... his ways... his habits... what he eats... when he sleeps. This monk can tell Jonah more about the giant and how to proceed."

Then the two men talked more about Jonah, and how the youth might go about getting a feather with the monk's help.

CHAPTER 10
DR. SANO VISITS JONAH

THE NEXT DAY a messenger from the King's court, accompanied by Dr. Sano, visited Jonah's home. The messenger knocked on the door and introduced himself and the doctor to Jonah's parents. They were mystified seeing visitors from the King, and surprised by Dr. Sano's peculiar appearance and garish clothing. But they quickly welcomed the visitors into their home.

"Please sit, how can we help you," said Jonah's father as he pointed to chairs.

The doctor sat down. "I'm sorry to trouble you and your family, but as you know our King has become terribly sick. However, we have recently learned of a cure for his sickness from a rhyme."

"A rhyme?" asked Jonah's father looking puzzled.

"Yes, a rhyme, sort of a riddle, a sorcerer's riddle. According to it, we need a feather from the giant who lives past the forest. The feather may be the only chance we have to save our King Leo."

Jonah's mother sat up straight in her chair, and sounding a little concerned asked, "What does this have to do with us?"

Now the doctor looked over at Jonah. "The King believes you, Jonah, can get a feather for him. He knows you are a very clever young man and trusts in you."

Jonah's eyebrows arched. He thought, *Me? Seriously?*

His father quickly protested, "Taking a feather from the giant is impossible."

Jonah's mother was stunned. She stood. "You can't be serious, Jonah can't possibly do this. No one can," she argued.

Gently, the doctor interrupted, "Yes, *taking* a feather from the giant may be impossible, but *finding* one may be possible. You see, there is a monk who lives at the monastery just beyond our village. He knows much about the giant and how he lives. This monk often spies on the giant from a treetop nest that he built near the giant's home and vineyard."

Jonah's parents looked a little relieved, but still had some concerns.

The doctor turned to face Jonah again. "Jonah, please visit this monk at the monastery and he will tell you how to find a feather." He extended his hand toward Jonah. "Give the monk this note from the King. When he reads this note, the monk will let you in, and help you find a feather."

Jonah took the note. "Who is this monk, and why is he so interested in the giant?"

"The monk's name is Brother Thomas," replied the doctor. "That's all I know, and the King did not explain any more than what I've told you."

Jonah stared at the note and looked uneasy.

"Jonah," continued the doctor, "you don't have to decide now, but at least go and visit with Brother Thomas at the monastery. Just listen to what he says about finding a feather. One feather, that's all we need. And remember saving the King will also save our kingdom. King Leo's two sons are both mysteriously missing for a year now. Should the King die there is no heir to the throne, and for certain there will be a war among the knights for power."

Jonah considered what a war would mean to the town, and about the good King's kindness and generosity. But he still looked unsure. His gaze drifted down and he stared at the note.

Dr. Sano appeared impatient and implored, "My friend, no one will fault you if you fail to return with a feather. The only failure is failure to try."

Jonah thought silently for a few moments, looking overwhelmed and uncertain how to respond.

The doctor was still and quietly waited, as he let Jonah ponder the situation.

A moment passed.

Jonah began to slightly nod his head, as he considered the options, risks, and loyalty to their generous King.

Dr. Sano noticed and half smiled.

Finally, Jonah decided. His optimistic and courageous nature rose to the challenge.

"Ok, I'll visit the monk, and at least find out what he has to say. I'll try my best for King Leo."

The doctor smiled. "That's all the King has asked, but he believes somehow you will be successful. Let's hope you are." His mood turned more serious. "And Jonah, please do not delay, the King's health continues to deteriorate. Thank you, and God's speed be with you." Dr. Sano said good night and left.

The next day Jonah's parents helped him prepare for his ride to the monastery. His father fitted new horseshoes on Jonah's horse Shadow, thinking the ride to the monastery might be just the beginning of Jonah's journey to find a feather. And Shadow was the name his mother had picked for this horse that Jonah had won in the King's contest. Everyone agreed there was no better name for the horse.

It was a clear afternoon, and Jonah was now ready to leave. As he mounted Shadow, his parents said goodbye and pleaded with Jonah to be careful. His parents stood close to each other as they watched their son ride off toward the monastery, and into what could be an important but perilous venture.

CHAPTER 11

ADVICE FROM A MONK AND A RABBI

Jonah and Shadow rode for a while, and then stopped briefly to drink some water from a quiet stream. As his horse drank, Jonah kneeled down and bent over to sip some water too. While drinking from the stream, he saw on the surface of the water the reflection of a feather floating just above his head. Jonah watched as the feather fell down and began to float in the stream. He reached out and grabbed it from the water. Jonah thought, *Well, it's just a sparrow's feather, but maybe it's a good omen. I'll hang onto it for good luck.* And he stuck the feather in his shirt for safekeeping.

But Jonah sat for some time by the stream, and fears of the unknown grew in his mind. He considered turning back, but remembered Dr. Sano's words that *the only failure is failure to try.* Jonah knew he had to at least visit the monk and find out more, so he hopped back onto Shadow and continued on.

It was now late afternoon, and a full moon was dimly visible in the pale blue sky. As Jonah rode, the moon seemed to play hide-and-seek with him, as it disappeared and appeared from behind large puffy clouds. Finally, Jonah reached a long path leading to the monastery entrance and rode up to the front door. He jumped off his horse, walked up the steps and knocked on the heavy wooden door. A robust man, the monastery caretaker, opened the door.

"Yes, how can we help you?" He asked sternly.

"My name is Jonah Paladin, and the King has sent me to meet with Brother Thomas. Please read this note signed by the King, and stamped with his wax seal."

The caretaker read the note Jonah handed him. Then he looked up at Jonah and eyed him carefully before finally opening the door fully. Jonah entered and the caretaker called for the monk. "Brother Thomas, we have a visitor."

Brother Thomas, a tall, lanky man entered the room wearing a brown robe and leaning on a cane as he walked.

The caretaker handed Brother Thomas the note. "This young man, Jonah Paladin, has just delivered this note from King Leo."

The monk read the note, and then looked up at Jonah. "Hmmm… a sorcerer's riddle. And a challenge to find a feather. Well, it's certainly a relief to learn that there may finally be a way to help King Leo. Everyone is very distressed over his poor health."

Brother Thomas extended a calloused bony hand, and delivered a handshake that gripped Jonah's hand tightly. While staring hard into Jonah's eyes, he slowly relaxed his grip before finally letting go and saying, "Nice to meet you Jonah."

Then the monk turned and walked across the room. He groaned slightly as he sat in a chair by a table. "I need to stay off my leg, as it was injured a few weeks ago, and may now be a little infected as well." He pointed to another chair. "Please sit here next to me Jonah."

Jonah sat next to Brother Thomas, but was a bit startled by what his host did next. The monk leaned over and squeezed Jonah's arms a little, as if to see how muscular they were. When he finished, the monk frowned and looked away.

Surprised and annoyed, Jonah frowned right back, but was also a little concerned about the monk's interest in his strength. For Jonah, much of the last few years were spent studying at school. And although he played classic harpastum ball games at school, let's just say no one would mistake skinny Jonah for an athlete.

As they sat close to each other, Brother Thomas began to tell Jonah that he knows a great deal about the giant. He explained that a feather could possibly cure the King, and that once the giant seemed to have mended a horse's injury with a feather.

Jonah was listening, but soon became distracted and started gazing across the room at something that caught his attention. It was a man quietly writing at a desk in a dark corner of the room. A single large candle lit the desk, and there were many open books stacked on it, and scattered on the floor around the man as well.

Brother Thomas quickly noticed that Jonah was distracted. The monk stopped speaking and firmly poked Jonah in the chest. "Ok, look at me, I need your attention. So, let me first satisfy your curiosity about that man writing in the room's corner. He is Rabbi Mortichai, a scholar and friend of mine who is here helping us translate Persian and Hebrew books into Latin. Now please pay attention to what I am telling you about the giant." The monk continued, "For some time now, I have watched the giant's habits closely. He lives beyond the forest in a round house surrounded by a maze made of vineyard fencing. The maze is quite complex and beautiful. And it's large, and clearly in-tended to keep people from reaching his house, which is located at the center of the maze. First, Jonah, you must understand..."

Unexpectedly, Rabbi Mortichai abruptly stood, turned around, and raised his hand to politely interrupt Brother Thomas in mid-sentence. The rabbi walked into the light, and Jonah could see that the man had a large beard, and wore a long black coat and a round fur hat. And the rabbi's fingers were heavily ink stained, apparently from writing.

Rabbi Mortichai walked over to Jonah and came uncomfortably close. He was holding some paper, ink and a horsehair pencil. "Jonah, our Brother Thomas will be telling you much. Write it down," he insisted sharply. The rabbi placed the paper and ink on the table near Jonah, dipped the horsehair pencil into the ink, and handed it to Jonah. "There is an old saying," he continued, "the dullest pencil has a better memory than the sharpest mind." Then the rabbi quietly returned to his corner desk, and resumed his work.

"Thank you Mortichai," Brother Thomas said, and then restarted his sentence. "First, Jonah, you must understand that the giant lives where he does so that no one can easily find him. His vineyard maze and house are located beyond a dense forest, an enchanted forest, as we all know. There are many strange and mystical creatures there. Some are good, some bad, and a few can be evil. Without any doubt, the forest has its perils. These perils keep most people from traveling deeply into the forest, and keep people away from the giant's home. That is his intention."

Jonah nodded.

The monk continued, "As you may know, Jonah, this forest is home to Saggio, a troublesome and very clever sorcerer. He is a handsome young man. But don't be fooled by his charm and good looks. It's been said that the prince-of-darkness comes well dressed as a gentleman. This sorcerer is so charming and clever that some say he can steal the soles right from under your shoes, or the gold from your teeth without even using his witchcraft. He lives in a hut at the heart of the forest. To keep people away, his hut has a sign above its door that welcomes no one. Jonah, you'll have to travel through this treacherous forest to reach the giant's vineyard maze, but stay as far away from the sorcerer's hut as you can. Your best hope to avoid the sorcerer, and the hazards and creatures of the forest rests among..." Brother Thomas paused, pointed up with a finger and then continued. "...the treetops."

Jonah looked puzzled. He stopped writing, looked up at the monk and skeptically asked, "My best hope rests among the treetops?"

Brother Thomas answered, "Yes, the treetops. Let me explain. The trees are very close in this old and dense forest. Their branches reach each other creating kind of a wooden web you can climb through. You must climb the trees and travel across the top of this forest, high above Saggio and other problems below on the ground. You will need to reach out for branches from treetop to treetop. I have done this many times, at least until my leg was injured." He lifted his cane. "Climbing is very slow and difficult for me now. At least until my leg is better." Brother Thomas lightly patted his thigh where the giant's arrow had struck him while up in his nest. But the monk did not explain the cause of his leg injury to Jonah.

The monk spent some time giving Jonah a few tips on how to climb across the tree branches. Explaining when to push with legs instead of pulling with arms, and how to judge when a branch is too thin to support his weight.

Jonah listened and kept writing it all down.

"Jonah, you'll have to learn the rest by doing it yourself. At first, you'll be as clumsy as a fat hog on wet ice. But you'll get better at climbing across tree-tops with practice, and you'll learn by your mistakes up there too. And just like a cat that jumps on a hot stove, you won't make the same mistake twice," he said with a laugh. Then his smile disappeared, as it was clear some other thought interrupted his humor. The monk's eyes scanned Jonah's arms again, and looked troubled as he squeezed the lad's arms for a second time.

Jonah looked irritated as the monk gripped his arms again, but didn't say anything and worried that he might not have sufficient strength for this arduous climb across the treetops.

"Jonah, you will need to start your climb by a certain pine tree. Don't worry, before you start your journey, I'll show you the tree's general direction from here. Also, I carved a large cross into its trunk, you can't miss it. Climb that pine tree to the top and you'll see some knives that I hammered into branches on that tree and other nearby trees. Follow the knives and they will get you climbing in the right direction toward the giant's vineyard."

From his desk and without looking up, Rabbi Mortichai loudly interjected, "Grab the handles not the blades."

Jonah looked up, smiled, and nodded.

"Yes, good point Mortichai. Jonah, at times you may be off balance as you climb, and looking ahead for the next branch, so don't grab knives too swiftly and find out you grabbed the wrong part the hard way." The monk raised his hand to show Jonah a scar in his palm.

Jonah looked but said nothing.

The monk continued. "Jonah, then after climbing across the treetops for a few hours, you'll reach the end of the forest, and the giant's large vineyard will be in your view. Look for the giant, who is almost always working in his vineyard maze. If you look from the treetops you will find him. But stay away from him and try not to let him see you."

Jonah wrote everything down.

"At times he rests in one of the chairs on his front porch. You need to know something about these chairs. There are two chairs. One is a rocking chair and the other is a straight-back table chair. If he's sitting in the table chair, he's taking a short rest and will return to work in the vineyard. If you see him in the rocking chair, he'll sit for a while then go into his house and won't come out again until the next day. That would be a very good time to search the vineyard for a feather."

Jonah was feeling more confident as he learned about the giant's habits, and knowing that the monk had already made many trips to the vineyard.

Brother Thomas added, "Of course, enter the maze quietly. You should be able to search the vineyard maze for a feather that has fallen off the giant, just as birds sometimes lose their feathers... and well... we our hair." The monk pointed to his own baldhead.

The youthful Jonah chuckled as he glanced up at the monk's baldhead. But then cringed a little and awkwardly apologized. "Oh, ummm, excuse me Brother."

The monk smiled. "You're fine Jonah, no worries."

"Sorry, but Brother Thomas, I do have a question."

The monk nodded.

"I'm not trying to split hairs... ummm... sorry again. But how will I know the giant's feathers from bird feathers that might be on the ground."

"Jonah, you're asking the right question. The giant's feathers are very small and gray with three black spots at the tip. And Jonah, don't start your search too late in the day, you will need some time and light to find a feather of course. And be careful not to get lost in the maze, it's large and complex."

Jonah nodded and kept writing.

Brother Thomas then began to describe the giant's appearance. "Jonah, try not to be alarmed by the looks of this creature. You see, he has some unusual features. He has a rather large nose. It's nothing like a bird's beak, it's more like a big round turnip. And he has one long tooth that hangs down, like a long spike, instead of a normal eyetooth." He pointed to his own eyetooth to illustrate. "But this long tooth is twisted like a corkscrew. I've seen him use it to crack open walnuts, yank out small bent nails, and even pull out corks from wine bottles. And he is a very big and imposing fellow, but not really a *giant* as many people call him."

Reaching under the table for a backpack, Brother Thomas opened it and checked its contents. "Take this backpack, Jonah, it has bread, nuts, fruit and cider. You'll need some food for the trip tomorrow morning, tonight you need to stay here. It's much too late for you to start your climb now."

The monk hesitated for a moment, but knew he had to continue and explain his nest... the good and the bad.

"Also Jonah, there is one last thing. After climbing across the forest to reach the giant's vineyard, you will be tired. You can rest in a nest that I made of branches and sheepskins. The nest is at the top of the highest tree at the edge of the giant's vineyard. It's a very tall elm tree." He paused and cleared his throat. "Jonah, you should also know that once, and only once mind you, the giant shot arrows at my nest."

Jonah listened and squinted, but kept writing.

"And one arrow did strike… my leg."

Jonah stopped writing. He froze.

"I was hurt, but able to climb back here." The monk laughed. "And I foolishly thought I might die that day. Well, anyway, I reinforced the nest with tree bark to protect myself from his arrows, but he never shot arrows after that one time."

Jonah dropped his horsehair pencil and looked alarmed. His eyes shot up from the paper.

"The giant shot an arrow into your leg!" Jonah pointed to the monk's injury.

"Relax Jonah, the giant saw me in the nest a few times after that and left me alone. He had a lapse of judgment on that one day only. I know him, and I'm certain it won't happen again."

The monk changed the subject. "Jonah, your arms are not very well developed, but you're thin and light, that's good for climbing. Actually, you're a lot like I was when I first started climbing, except you're much younger than me. And that's good." He smiled at Jonah. "You'll be able to withstand the ordeal just fine."

"Ok, that's encouraging to hear Brother Thomas. But let's go back to that arrow part." Jonah looked uneasy and worried.

Brother Thomas looked calm and unconcerned. "It won't happen again Jonah. I'm sure of this. And as I said, my nest is now lined with tree bark and safe, no arrow can penetrate. Jonah, I would not let you go if I thought arrows were a danger to you."

Jonah was quiet. A moment passed and he began to feel a little reassured.

"Look, it's getting late Jonah. Let's have a quick meal, and we can talk further as we eat. Are you hungry Jonah?"

"Yes, I could eat, thank you Brother Thomas." He smiled.

When the monk stood and turned toward a cabinet, Jonah softly whispered to himself, "fiducia."

The monk heard Jonah, and quickly turned back around. He grinned. "I see you know some Latin." He paused and then added, "Jonah, you will also need... *dura.*"

Jonah looked at Brother Thomas for an explanation.

"Dura is the Latin word for endurance," answered the monk. "You will need both physical and mental endurance. You will need to remain dedicated and persevere."

Jonah had some concerns, but regained his confidence. He replied, "fiducia, dura."

The monk nodded. "Exactly, you will need both confidence and endurance." He paused. "Are you still ok with all of this?"

"Ummm… yes, I'm still on board." Jonah smiled.

"Great. And Jonah, if you run into trouble, you can always turn back and return here. We are all just happy you are willing to try and help."

Jonah nodded.

"Thank you Jonah." Brother Thomas put his hand on Jonah's shoulder. He was very grateful.

After the three finished their meal, the caretaker showed Jonah to his bedroom for the night. He left Jonah by the door of a guest room, and continued down the hall to his own room. But Jonah followed him to ask about Brother Thomas. Jonah was curious to know why the monk was so interested in the giant. However, before Jonah could ask, the caretaker entered his room and slammed the door behind himself, seemingly unaware Jonah was standing just outside his doorway.

In the hall outside the room, Jonah could hear the caretaker say something. It sounded to Jonah that he mumbled something about the return of someone named Julia. Jonah gently knocked on the door.

Instantly, the door flew open and the caretaker appeared. So quickly that it startled Jonah for a moment, but he showed no alarm.

"Sir, may I ask you something about the monk?"

The caretaker answered only with a stare.

Nevertheless, Jonah asked, "Why is the monk so interested in the giant?"

The caretaker looked away. "Brother Thomas knows him," he answered and closed the door on Jonah.

Now Jonah was even more curious. "But how? How could Brother Thomas know the giant? When did they meet?" But no answer came from behind the closed door.

Jonah had many other questions, like, where did the giant come from, and who else might know him? Has the caretaker met him? And Jonah also wanted to know who Julia was, but stopped himself from asking and walked back to his guest room. Inside, Jonah undressed and went to bed, but lay there awake for some time just staring into the darkness of the room. The more he thought, the more his questions grew and gathered in his mind, and seemed to swarm like harassing hornets. Late that night, exhausted, Jonah finally fell asleep.

The next morning Jonah took the backpack prepared by Brother Thomas, and stepped outside to begin his trip. Brother Thomas, Rabbi Mortichai and the care-taker were already outside waiting for him. Jonah said goodbye to them, and looked confident but a little tense.

Brother Thomas sensed the lad's concern. "Jonah, the good news is, I've survived this trip many times, even my first inexperienced journey. You'll be just fine."

Jonah nodded, smiled and looked more confident.

Rabbi Mortichai added, "The bad news is, there is no lifeguard on duty, so be careful."

Jonah nodded, turned and started walking toward the forest, but after a few steps looked back over his shoulder and reminded the men, "And take good care of Shadow until I return, Ok?"

The monk replied, "Of course," as the three men watched Jonah begin his daunting journey toward the forest.

Moments passed.

The men stood silently as they watched Jonah disappear into the distance.

The rabbi quietly muttered, "Jonah's search for a feather is like a fishing line blindly cast at night into a black and sinister sea. One may unluckily reel in a monster and not a fish."

The monk shot a look at him. "I don't think it will be that bad."

"No? I pray you are correct Thomas."

CHAPTER 12

WELCOME NO ONE.
EVIL INSIDE.

Jonah left the monastery and hiked until he reached the start of the forest. He looked around and quickly spotted the pine tree with the cross carved into its trunk, just as Brother Thomas had described.

Like a toddler taking its first few steps, Jonah slowly began his climb to the top of the forest. Halfway up the tree he stopped for a short time to gather his thoughts and briefly considered turning back. Stress and worry were clouding this mind. Then from his pocket he pulled the notes he had written down while Brother Thomas explained how to proceed and what to expect. Just reading the notes made Jonah feel more confident and reassured. *Glad I wrote all this stuff down. Maybe I didn't have a choice,* he thought as Jonah remembered how Rabbi Mortichai handed him the horsehair pencil. *I'm Ok, just need to keep moving.* And Jonah kept climbing up.

Jonah looked around as he climbed. The forest's scenery was so beautiful that it was visually intoxicating as the season was autumn and leaf colors were bright yellows and reds. Climbing among these brilliant leaves, Jonah imagined that he had stepped into a vast painting splashed with dazzling colors. He climbed until he reached the treetop where he vanished from sight as if slowly swallowed up by a leafy sea.

A moment later, Jonah saw something up ahead, and barely visible through the dense tree foliage. He saw branches with the knives hammered into them by the monk. *I simply need to follow the knives now.* He reached for the first knife thinking, *Grab the handles not the blades.* Jonah then began climbing across the treetops reaching for knives and moving toward his destination. As he climbed, Jonah felt the constant tug of gravity on his body. Remembering the monk's advice, Jonah tried to rely on his leg muscles to push his body as he climbed. This helped save the strength in his arms. He continued along the treetops reaching out from branch to branch, and grabbing knives whenever he saw them. But now Jonah took hold of the last knife. There were no others up ahead, and Jonah would now be on his own to stay on course for the giant's vineyard.

An hour of hard climbing had passed. "Now what am I supposed to do," Jonah said out loud, "my legs and arms are all pretty tired." Jonah found a curved branch to sit on and rest. The branch offered a rounded but narrow seat. Jonah rested for a while before starting out again. But he moved too quickly and lost his grip. Jonah began to fall! Fear shot through his mind as he fell headfirst banging into branches and plummeting down. With his arms flying around wildly searching for a branch to grab onto, he looked like he was fighting off bees. Luckily his leg caught a branch in this dense forest.

As Jonah hung upside down by a leg, his mind raced. The brief fall was so fast that Jonah wasn't even sure what had happened. "Did my leg catch the branch, or did the branch catch my leg?" After hanging there for a few seconds, he managed to grab hold of a branch and pull his body upright. "I have to be more careful... No lifeguard on duty." He carefully sat on the branch and rested. He was a little shaken but otherwise all right. Jonah calmed himself down and collected his thoughts. "Fiducia, dura... confidence, endurance," he said, "I can make it." Jonah reached out and slowly resumed his climb. He was back on track and a little more skilled as he headed toward the giant's vineyard.

From branch to branch, tree after tree, Jonah continued. Then a different kind of tree was ahead. It looked like a huge fruit tree. *A pear tree?* he wondered. Jonah climbed over to it, and sure enough, there were pears. Big, juicy pears. He reached for one, pulled if off the branch, and bit into it. Then instantly, as if from nowhere, a large bird landed right in front of him. It was a partridge. Jonah recalled a verse from a very old Christmas poem "...a partridge perched in a pear tree, for all the Saints to sing and see." Then another bird landed. It too was a partridge. Then others, then many, then hundreds. So many birds had come that Jonah couldn't even move to another branch. Fluttering wings were everywhere. Jonah couldn't see anything but birds and feathers. And next, birds began landing on him too. Jonah dropped the pear he was eating and swung his arms to chase away the birds. But in the chaos Jonah lost his balance and again began to fall! He fell and fell, hitting branches and tumbling through a mass of birds. A small hut was right below and Jonah fell onto its soft thatched roof breaking his fall, and weakening the blow. He rolled off the roof, falling onto the ground. Jonah was dazed but unhurt. When Jonah opened his eyes, he saw right in front of his face the half-eaten pear that he dropped. "Aarrg… lost my appetite," he grunted.

Jonah stood up and brushed himself off. Then he looked up and saw the hut's front door and a sign above it. The sign read…

Welcome No One. Evil Inside.

Jonah thought, *This must be the hut of Saggio the sorcerer that Brother Thomas warned me about. No time to waste, better get out of here before I'm found.* As Jonah ran away from the hut, he was unaware that the smiling Saggio was watching him from behind a window… the whole time.

CHAPTER 13

LETTERS THAT MAKE SAGGIO LAUGH

FROM HIS WINDOW, Saggio watched Jonah run off until the lad disappeared among the trees. Saggio stepped back from his window and sat in a chair to read his mail. He tore open the first envelope.

"Ahh, this looks like a nice 'thank you' letter from a customer who appreciates by magical talents." Saggio read....

Dear Sorcerer Saggio,

Before you cast your spell, my wife hated my baldhead, and called me such horrid names as 'stone-head, 'melon-mound' and so on. But now she loves to kiss and caress it, while saying it's her whole world and her magic moon.

Thank you Sir Saggio,
Joe the barber

Saggio chuckled, "That's a very nice letter, let's see what's in the next envelop," as he tore it open.

To Saggio the Imbecile,

I paid you to cast a thousand wounds on my neighbor's farm so that the owner, a swine of a man, would suffer and starve. Saggio, you are the worst incompetent. Your ears must be as deaf as mushrooms. I said to cast *wounds* not *tombs!* After your spell was cast, the farmer discovered an ancient catacomb beneath his land while digging a deep well. Buried in the catacomb are a thousand ancient tombs of people from all walks of life... celebrated citizens, slaves and saints. So now, the Church has paid this farmer a fortune in gold for his property. And the Bishop will preserve the catacomb and build a cathedral to rest above it! The cata-comb will be named after this farmer, a pig of a man who I curse every day with every breath I take. Saggio, return my payment in full, so that I may hire a competent sorcerer. I will look for an ugly one, and should have not trusted your good looks and charms.

Many regrets,
Tim the tiller

Saggio smirking, "He wants his money back? Don't make me laugh! What does he think, I run a fish market? He should have made friends with the farmer who might have now shared his newfound wealth with him." Saggio then tapped a finger on the customer's signature, saying, "And take the marbles out of your mouth, sir, no one can understand a word you are saying. Unbelievable... *wounds... tombs...* this Tim is a tongue-tied lout! Next letter..."

Dear Saggio,

A youth named, Jonah Paladin, is traveling through your forest. You'll find him climbing among the trees, up high above the ground. I enclose twelve gold coins in payment to ensure he does not safely reach his destination.

Thank you,
Malvagio the stable-master

Saggio beamed and burst out laughing. "Ha ha, getting paid for something I'm already working on for my own purposes. What's better than this!" Saggio rattled the coins in his two fists while he cackled with laughter. "This is too good to be true, old Malvagio is giving me money for my little 'Jonah project' that I've already started! Poor Jonah doesn't know what he's in for, or even know why I'm pestering him with birds, and more trouble soon on its way."

CHAPTER 14
FAYRISSA OF HIBERNIA

JONAH RAN FROM SAGGIO'S HUT for some time before he resumed climbing up a tree. He leaped up and onto a low branch and began his ascent. He reached the treetop and was greeted by a perfectly blue sky. He could hear the sweet sound of birds singing in the distant forest. Sparrows, finches, blue-jays and others softly chirped. The forest was peaceful and the weather was perfect.

Jonah was calm. "Looks like my troubles are behind me. I got past the sorcerer's hut, and I'm now more than half way across the forest."

But then suddenly, all the birds quickly stopped singing. Instantly, Jonah realized there was some problem in the forest. He thought, *Something is wrong, why did they all stop singing so abruptly?* He stopped climbing and looked around to see what the trouble was.

"This isn't good. Something isn't right."

Jonah correctly understood the birds' warning. In a flash, the sky swiftly darkened. And from nowhere a massive rainstorm descended on Jonah. The wind swirled and the rain gushed down on him. The hard rain hurt as it struck his face. Jonah was instantly soaked. His wet hands made it difficult to keep a good grip on the branches, so he climbed more slowly and deliberately.

I have to stay up here and keep climbing, Jonah thought. *I have to get farther away from that sorcerer's hut. Only bad things can come from Saggio's hut.* Jonah was right, but he didn't realize how right.

After a few more minutes the storm quickly passed. The rain stopped, the clouds vanished, and now the sun shone very brightly. Up in the treetops, Jonah's clothes started to dry in the hot sun faster than dewdrops in a desert. Then the wind came. It was an intensely hot sirocco from the south. The sun beat down and the hot wind blew wildly. After a short time, Jonah felt he would waste away like a burning candle if he didn't climb down to the ground to seek shelter from the hot sunshine. As Jonah climbed down branches through the heat, he saw a steamy fog forming close to the ground caused by the sun's strong heat on the rainwater. He continued climbing down until his legs disappeared into the fog below. Then through a clear patch of fog Jonah saw a large rock just beneath him. From a low branch he leaped down onto the rock and laid face down to rest for a moment. *I need to get out of this scorching wicked weather,* he thought. Then something happened. *Is this rock moving?* It definitely was! The rock was slowly moving. Alarmed, Jonah sat up and looked around, "Ohhh…. this isn't a rock at all. I'm on the back of a large tortoise!" Jonah saw that the tortoise was heading toward a very large tree with a big hollow opening at the base of its trunk, and so he stayed on its back. *I've heard of these huge trees, but never saw one. It should be much cooler inside the tree.*

The tree trunk was as big as a small house, and its opening was as big as a door. Jonah, riding atop the tortoise, passed through the tree's entrance. It was cool inside the tree's hollow trunk. But Jonah noticed dim candlelight flickering. It was coming from a large hole in the ground. Jonah stepped off the tortoise and looking down the hole, he saw a ladder.

He heard a woman's voice gently beckon, "One hundred thousand welcomes. Please come in."

Jonah carefully approached the hole. He looked down, and deciding it looked safe, he then slowly began to climb down the ladder.

Jonah saw an old woman dressed in shabby clothing standing and painting at an artist's easel. "Come in, come in," she said, as she waved her skinny hand.

"It's quite safe in here. And much cooler than being outside in that fiery sirocco."

Jonah stepped off the bottom on the ladder.

She turned her old weathered face toward Jonah. "My goodness it is hot and dry today, and a drink of anything would be very welcome. I'm very thirsty and parched."

Jonah felt sorry for the old woman. "I have some cider, would you care for some?"

"That would be wonderful, thank you for your generosity."

Jonah smiled, reached into his backpack and pulled out a jug of cider. He pulled out the cork, poured cider into a cup, and offered it to the old woman.

She took a long drink. "Thank you, the hot weather is dreadful." She handed the cup back with a broad smile.

Jonah looked down to return the jug and cup into his backpack, and in the twinkling of an eye the old woman was transformed. When Jonah looked back at her, standing before him was a beautiful woman in a glossy green gown.

Her radiant eyes sparkled like two bright blue topaz gems. She laughed. "Don't be frightened, I was just playing in one of my favorite disguises. As I said before, it's safe down here. And thank you again for the cider."

Jonah was a little alarmed, but he had already seen a few other mystical events in this enchanted forest, and had heard much about the magic here.

"What are you painting?" he asked politely, as he cautiously looked around at the same time.

"Well, what do you think I'm painting?" as the woman turned back around to face the easel again.

"Uhhh, well, it's an unusual painting. It looks like lots of different colored *zeros*."

The woman laughed and shook her head, her long straight hair flowing back and forth.

Jonah guessed again, "Well, is this a painting of letter *O's* perhaps?"

She laughed again. "You're thinking much too much," she answered while painting.

Jonah was baffled and offered no other answers.

Then, this mysterious woman stopped painting, faced Jonah again and explained. "These are just little colored circles, not number *zeros*, not letter *O's*. I'm just drawing circles. Some are close to perfect circles, but it's hard to do. Want to try?"

"Oh, no, no thanks. I'm a terrible artist," confessed Jonah.

She continued, "I like circles, they are endless lines that go on and on forever. Life is a circle. The circle of life is… birth, death, then rebirth in the afterlife. And so many beautiful things are circles… like the sun and moon, and rings and things, and buttons and balls children play with."

Then she picked up a harp that was behind the easel and breathed softly across its strings, which began to vibrate. She sang a melody and the harp began to play the tune. She began to dance, and as she did her straight hair swirled around and turned into long soft curls that bounced up and down in rhythm with her dancing feet. Sometimes her legs kicked high. Her toes tapped, and at times her feet stamped down a beat to the lively music.

After seeing the harp play by itself, Jonah was a bit more concerned, and wanted to know more about this mystical woman.

"May I ask who you are?"

"I am Fayrissa the Forest Sprite," she answered while still dancing. "I come from far away, from the Woods of Duiblinn in Hibernia, a beautiful land of cool breezes and rolling hills covered with soft green grass, much greener than any green you can paint or even imagine. And as for you… who are you?"

"I'm Jonah Paladin. And I'm in search of a feather from the feathered giant who lives past the forest."

Nodding as she continued dancing, "Yes, I know."

A moment later, Fayrissa stopped her dance, and the music stopped too. Standing and facing Jonah, she added, "And you my young man are on a very worthy, but difficult quest. Good luck to you. I must leave now and get myself ready for a brief visit to Duiblinn, but I will return soon."

In a flash, she disappeared into a bright cloud of smoke that twinkled like sunshine sprinkled with green emerald dust. Whereupon, Fayrissa, her harp, and her painting were all gone.

CHAPTER 15

STEPPING INTO A MUSIC BOX

JONAH LEFT THE HOLLOW OF THE TREE now that the heat and wind had stopped. He wondered about Fayrissa as he continued on his way climbing across the forest's treetops. Then his hand brushed a very large leaf on the tree he had just climbed onto. To his great surprise, a single musical note rang out from the leaf. With eyes wide open, Jonah watched as the leaf swung back and forth while it rang like a chime. The leaf hit another leaf that rang another note. These two leaves hit two other leaves that also rang. Now there were four ringing leaves. These four ringing leaves hit four others, and now these eight ringing leaves hit eight others, and so on. Jonah thought, *This is what my math teacher called 'exponential growth.'* Then in a flash, thousands of leaves on the tree were ringing like chimes and sounding like instruments tuning up for a concert. Then the tree's leaves sounded more in harmony and soon a beautiful melody arose. The tree was like a huge music box that Jonah could watch and listen to from within.

Jonah rested and listened to the ringing music for a few minutes watching the leaves sway back and forth. But soon the music started to sound a little off-key. Then the leaves started sounding less like music and more like harsh noise that grew louder as each second passed. Rapidly, the notes fused together into a blasting roar, and Jonah had to cover his ears with both hands while sitting on a branch. He couldn't move. His hands were protecting his ears from the loud and deafening madness. Jonah didn't know what to do next. He helplessly sat there wishing it would stop soon.

Nearby in the forest, Fayrissa was cracking walnuts and feeding a group of squirrels. She was giving them a treat before she left for her trip to Duiblinn. Then Fayrissa noticed a loud racket in the distance.

"That young fellow, Jonah, is in trouble again. And that sorcerer, Saggio, is to blame I'm sure." She looked around and saw the top of a quivering tree that blasted out noise in every direction.

She pointed at two fluffy squirrels, "You two. Nico and Pico. Go and help Jonah. You'll know what to do."

The two little creatures dashed across the woods and then finally up into the noisy tree where they found Jonah holding both his ears. The two jumped on top of Jonah's head, and grabbed hold of his hair. Jonah was startled and reached up to push them away. Hanging from his hair, the squirrels swung down to the sides of his head where they shoved their furry bottoms straight into his ears. Poor Jonah didn't know what hit him, but soon realized these little creatures were trying to help him. Their fluffy bottoms covered his ears like earmuffs, protecting Jonah from the terribly loud cacophony, and freeing his hands for climbing. The two squirrels stayed on Jonah's head long enough for Jonah to climb to another tree. As soon as he left the musical tree, its terrible sound faded, and shortly after the tree fell totally silent.

The two squirrels jumped from Jonah and onto a nearby branch. Jonah was relieved and laughed at how he must have looked with squirrel bottoms stuffed into both of his ears.

"I don't know if you can understand this, but thank you," Jonah told them.

To his great surprise, one squirrel replied, "You're welcome Jonah. Fayrissa sent us to help you." The squirrel continued, "I am Nico and he is my cousin, Pico," pointing to his squirrel partner.

Looking closely at the two small creatures, Jonah was astonished that Nico spoke. Jonah had lots of questions, but this one came out first, "Squirrels have cousins?"

"Of course, why wouldn't we?" replied Nico.

Jonah shook his head. "I don't know, I guess I never thought about it."

Nico laughed. "But look at us, can't you see how much we look alike? Everyone says we almost look like twins."

Jonah chuckled, thinking how all squirrels look exactly alike, at least to humans.

Jonah looked closer at Nico and then looked at Pico. He saw no difference in their appearance, but politely replied, "Oh, now I see what you mean, now I see the special family resemblance that you two share."

Nico smiled, nodded and then added, "He and I are very similar except Pico never speaks."

"Is that because he's not able to speak, they way you can?" Jonah asked.

"Oh, no, he certainly can, but he's decided not to."

"You mean Pico is a talking squirrel who chooses not to talk? I can't even believe I actually just said that."

"Correct," answered Nico.

"And why is that?" Jonah questioned.

"You see, Jonah, we were adopted by Fayrissa who's given us the ability to speak so we can be better helpers.

However, Pico has realized that by not speaking he's more popular in the forest with other squirrels. A talking squirrel is really weird, and a really big turn-off to other squirrels. We sound nuts to them when we talk. Uhhh… no pun intended."

Jonah laughed, "I can only imagine."

"Ever since Pico stopped talking he has lots of friends. He's very popular, kind of like a little squirrel mayor now." Then Nico leaned closer to Jonah and whispered, "And Pico even has a girlfriend now too."

Jonah chuckled. "Oh, I see. But what about you, Nico, don't you want friends… and a girlfriend too?"

"I do have a few friends, but not many, because I just can't stop talking sometimes. I'm a very gregarious squirrel you see."

"Yes, I can see that." Jonah smiled and agreed.

"My best friend is my cousin, Pico. And I have a few other squirrel friends who don't seem to care a bit when I mess up and talk to them. They just accept that I'm a little weird," then Nico sighed, "and so does my girlfriend."

Jonah smiled. "Well, it's really great to have friends that accept you as you are, and just a few good friends is all anyone really needs."

Then Jonah looked up at the sky. "Well, it's getting late. It's been great chatting with you, but I have to get going. So, thank you very much, fellas, and thank Fayrissa for me as well."

"We will Jonah, and be well." Then Nico waved as the two fluffy critters scampered off into the woods.

Jonah continued climbing.

Fiducia, dura... confidence, endurance... he kept thinking.

CHAPTER 16

FINDING THE NEST, THE MAZE... AND MORE

THE DAY GREW LATE. Finally, Jonah was reaching the end of the forest. He could see there was a clearing beyond the trees where the giant's vineyard might be. Then he spotted a very tall elm tree that looked like it had a dense leafy top. He climbed toward it and spotted the monk's nest. To Jonah, the nest was like a beautiful leafy oasis. Jonah headed straight for the nest with his last burst of energy. Finally, he reached the nest's rim and let his tired body tumble down into its soft bottom where he rested for a long time.

After he rested, Jonah stood and looked down at the strange vineyard below. It twisted and turned with many paths leading to dead ends. It was a beautiful, but complex maze. At the middle of the maze he saw the giant's windowless, round house. The house and the maze were silent and perfectly still. Jonah saw and heard no one.

He reached into his backpack for a drink of cider. After a few sips, he looked around again, but this time he saw the giant sitting on the front porch of the house. He couldn't see any details of the giant, except that he looked like a large man. He stared for a few minutes and just watched him sitting, as Jonah wondered what he's like. Then Jonah realized, *He's sitting in the rocking chair... this means he's done working for the day and wont enter the vineyard. This is great! I have an opportunity to safely search the edges of the maze for a feather while the giant remains sitting far away.* Jonah checked his notes to be certain that the rocking chair, and not the table chair, meant the giant was done working for the day. If Jonah had that mixed up, it would be a very bad mistake.

Jonah descended the tree. And although his body ached from tree climbing, he started his search at the edge of the maze for a feather. It was getting late, so he hoped he could find a feather soon, and return to the nest to sleep and then start his trip back at sunrise. "This may be a lot easier than anyone had thought.

All I need is one feather." But suddenly, Jonah heard a small twig brake. He quickly froze in his footsteps. He listened carefully, but heard nothing. "I only need one feather, and I'm gone." Then out of nowhere, Jonah felt something under his feet. "What the… ahhh, nooo!" Without knowing it, Jonah was standing on a large net that was hidden beneath some loose dirt and leaves. Jonah had stepped onto a trap, and was swiftly being whisked straight up into the air. The next thing Jonah knew, he was tangled in a net, suspended from a long branch, up high in a tree with no possible escape.

CHAPTER 17

A SORCERER AFFLICTED WITH AFFECTION

FLYING JUST ABOVE the forest's treetops, Fayrissa quickly made her way to the sorcerer's hut. After sending Nico and Pico to rescue Jonah from the deafening tree, she had decided to speak with Saggio before she left for her trip to Duiblinn.

From outside his door she called, "Saggio, come out, we need to talk," shaking her head as she looked up at the sign on his hut that welcomed no one.

Instantly, the dashing young sorcerer appeared, his face beaming with a smile from ear-to-ear. He was very fond of Fayrissa, but she wanted no part of him.

"Come in! Come in!" Saggio offered pleasantly, as he motioned with his hand.

"What about the sign on your hut, it says no one is welcome."

"Fayrissa, that's meant for the others around here, not you."

"No thanks, Saggio, I rather tell you what I have to say from out here."

"Oh, *pleeeease*, do come in, you're always welcome," Saggio pleaded. His skin tingled with anticipation.

Fayrissa stepped just inside his doorway, but no farther.

"Fayrissa, how can I help you? And may I say you look more beautiful each time I see you."

"Stop Saggio, you can't charm me with your words. I don't want to hear words. It's your deeds that I'm here about."

"Deeds?" replied Saggio trying to sound and look innocent.

"Yes. Deeds. I'm here about the trouble in the forest you have been causing for that young man, Jonah," Fayrissa complained.

"Oh that, those deeds. I don't mean to do him any harm, you know."

"Well, you're certainly causing him enough trouble. Birds, rain, heat, wind, music, noise."

"Ahhh, that's not real trouble," winked Saggio, "just some tricks."

"And why are you playing tricks on Jonah? What do you have to do with him?"

"Nothing," Saggio answered.

"Nothing?" she asked, doubting his answer.

"Nothing. To be honest, Fayrissa, I stirred up a little trouble for Jonah knowing it would bring you here. I just wanted to see you before your trip to Duiblinn, so we could chat and maybe have some tea together." Saggio's smile sparkled.

"What? Saggio, you've lost your mind! I want nothing to do with you or your evil witchcraft."

"Evil? You're hurting my feelings. I'm not evil," insisted Saggio.

"Yes you are," Fayrissa pointed a finger up, "even your sign outside says so. It says, *Welcome No One. Evil Inside.*"

"Fayrissa, that sign is there to keep the others in the forest from annoying me. I'm actually very nice, some say even charming," as he nodded while grinning.

"Look Saggio, you can't fool me with your lies and charm. I'm here to tell you to leave Jonah alone."

"You're here to *tell* me? Order me? Well, actually you, and only you Fayrissa, can give me orders."

"Saggio, I'm not ordering, but I am *asking* you, and I'm asking nicely."

"For you, my lovely Fayrissa, anything. Anyway, I'm done with my tricks on Jonah, I've already gotten what I wanted… which was a visit from you." Saggio smiled.

CHAPTER 18
A NEW PRISONER WITH NO ESCAPE

J ONAH STRUGGLED FURIOUSLY but could find no way out of the net that held him prisoner. He hung helplessly from a branch high above the ground for some time before finally falling asleep from exhaustion.

Time passed, Jonah got some needed rest. Then suddenly, Jonah's sleep was abruptly disturbed. The net was moving… it was being slowly lowered! Jonah awoke to a horror, as two large feathery arms roughly grabbed hold of the net with almost a crushing force. Instantly, Jonah knew his worst fears were realized… it was indeed the feathered giant who had trapped him!

The giant lifted Jonah up onto a large powerful plow horse. Tangled in a net, Jonah was dropped on the horse's back like a large sack of potatoes. The feathered giant had captured Jonah, and rode with his prisoner behind his saddle.

Jonah was terrified as he grasped the true horror of the situation. He cringed with regret as he realized, *I walked right into his trap, thinking it was totally safe just because the giant was in the rocking chair. How could I have been so stupid?* His head was throbbing. Jonah's plan had gone terribly wrong.

But as the horse trotted through the maze, Jonah was bouncing up and down on its back. And as the bouncing ride continued, Jonah thought at each quick turn in the maze that he might fall off. *If I fall off, I might get chance to run, that is, if I don't hurt myself in the fall.* Finally, at one turn the horse's bounce allowed Jonah to arch his back and slide off the horse and onto his feet. Jonah stumbled and struggled, but managed to unwrap the netting, and then ran as fast as he could without making too much noise. After a few random turns in the maze, Jonah picked up speed allowing his feet to stomp down with some noise. He could hear the horse's trot continue farther into the distance, with the giant unaware that Jonah had fallen off. Jonah kept running blindly through the maze hoping to find the entrance to the woods, but none appeared. He also knew that if he climbed over the vineyard fencing, the giant could easily see him.

Suddenly, Jonah heard the giant's horse start to gallop fast in his direction. The giant had discovered that his prisoner was gone. Jonah kept running and turning not knowing if he was advancing toward the woods or deeper into the maze. As the giant's horse came within a few turns of him, Jonah spotted an unusually thick section of leafy vine. He raced for it hoping the vine's dense leaves and the faint light of the late evening sky would prevent the giant from spotting him.

Jonah leaped into the leafy vines faster than a cat into a church on a stormy night. He froze among the leaves and held his breath knowing the giant was alarmingly close. Then he saw the horse's legs flash by his face. The giant had ridden past him! The feathered giant kept riding while looking everywhere, his eyes scanning for the intruder.

Next, the giant rode to where Jonah had entered the maze. He rode around the forest's edge for some time and then seemed to assume that this trespasser disappeared into the darkness of the woods. The giant returned to the maze, rode through it and back to his house.

Jonah stayed frozen in the leafy greenery until the night grew late and dark. Finally, he stood up, looked around and quickly concluded that his only way out of the maze was to climb the vineyard fencing and head straight to the woods under the cover of darkness.

After leaping over a dozen vine-covered fences, Jonah reached the woods and found his way to the tallest tree with the monk's nest at its top. He climbed up to the nest, dropped into it, let his tired body slip beneath a stack of sheepskins, and vanished from sight. Jonah slept quietly under that heap, and only the owls watched over his sleep.

The next day's crisp morning air, and bright sunrise broke Jonah's deep sleep. Now wakening, Jonah pulled his hands out from under the sheepskins, and used his warm palms to cover for a moment the cool skin of his face. He breathed deeply and opened his eyes.

Half asleep, Jonah slowly stood up in the nest and looked around. Still groggy from the night's sleep, he didn't know what to do next. Jonah saw no sign of the giant, but worried that the giant would return and resume searching for him.

As Jonah shook off the night's sleep and fully woke, his decision became clear… he would start climbing back to the monastery and admit his defeat. Jonah wasn't happy, but reasoned, *Well, at least I didn't fail to try.* He knew it was time to leave and head home. Jonah grabbed his backpack and lifted one leg over the nest's wall as he reached for a branch.

But then unexpectedly, a loud noise startled Jonah. His body jumped. At first, Jonah wasn't sure what he heard. The sound repeated. Jonah looked stunned. He distinctively heard a dog's bark. Jonah looked straight down. In total disbelief, Jonah saw a large black dog at the base of his tree!

Then in a flash, the giant stormed out of his hut. Jonah watched the giant mount his horse and race through the maze toward him. Jonah was paralyzed, as his eyes locked onto the rapidly approaching creature on horseback. There was no escape!

Jonah's breathing became more rapid. He felt his heart start to pound, and a slight sweat broke on his brow. Jonah knew that the unthinkable had become his reality. After escaping from the maze and thinking he was safe, Jonah was soon to be challenged by the hostile giant... face-to-face.

CHAPTER 19

OSCAR'S MANY BAD HABITS

FAYRISSA LEFT SAGGIO hoping that he would stop playing tricks on Jonah, as he had promised her. She took flight for Duiblinn. Upon her arrival, her sister Marissa greeted her.

"Welcome home my younger sister. It's been too long."

They embraced each other.

The two sisters sat and had tea as they caught up on news.

"So, Fayrissa, how is your Forest Sprite career going in them ol' woods down in Liguria?" Marissa asked.

"Just great, Marissa, I just love the valley and the forest, and the winters have been mild."

"And what about your personal life? Have you seen that handsome young Saggio lately? Any news there?" she asked with a friendly smile.

"News? Saggio and me? Is that what you mean? Oh, no, no… I can't stand the sight of him! He's so conceited, and a troublemaker too. Yesterday, he caused a ruckus in the forest just to trick me into visiting him, and that's not a way to a woman's heart."

Marissa poured more tea into both cups. "Maybe not. But you know, you're not getting any younger Fayrissa, and you seem to put all your energy into your career. Why not take some time for a relationship. You're almost two-hundred years old now, almost middle-age for a witch."

"I am not just a witch," Fayrissa shot back, "I'm now a Forest Sprite, and my career consumes all of my time. It's important that someone watches over the forest. I help wherever I can."

Marissa continued, "Sometimes I think you should have married that young warlock from Londinium years ago, before all this career stuff filled your head. Fayrissa, what was that warlock's name?"

"That was Oscar," replied Fayrissa and looking a little annoyed by the question.

"And why did you two break up again?" Marissa asked sipping her tea.

"We broke up because," Fayrissa paused as she looked up to think, "let's see… he had a very loud goofy laugh, broke everything he touched, and scratched his armpits a lot."

Marissa questioned, "Really? Was that Oscar? I thought Oscar was the one who chewed with his mouth open, was always sniffling and had very bad handwriting, like a first grader."

"Oh, yes, Oscar was all those things too," Fayrissa replied smiling and nodding her head briskly.

They both laughed, but Fayrissa stopped laughing first, and feeling self-conscious she gave a quick and final awkward smile.

"Well, Fayrissa, considering Oscar's bad habits, and the other strange men you've dated in the past, perhaps Saggio isn't all that bad," Marissa suggested.

Fayrissa glared, "Stop saying that Marissa! He's charming yes, and doesn't have icky personal habits, but he has no ethics. He'll take money from strangers in return for granting any curse or charm. That's not my style."

"Fayrissa, don't be so self-righteous, that's part of any sorcerer's business model. All this Forest Sprite stuff is making you too uptight."

"Don't give me that line, Marissa, my career is fine and my life is balanced. And also, you don't know how out of line Saggio can be." Fayrissa folded her arms across her chest, and looked away not wanting to continue.

Marissa understood, so she changed the topic, and the two began to chat again.

The ladies chatted all night, but Marissa tried to bring up Saggio once again during their conversation. Fayrissa interrupted her and finally said, "It's getting late, I'm tired and going to bed." And not wanting to sound impolite, but she said to her sister goodnight.

CHAPTER 20
THE FINAL FALL

RIDING HIS HORSE HARD, the giant sped through the maze. Soon he would be at the base of Jonah's tree and nest. Frantically, Jonah began to climb out of the nest and reached out for a branch on the next tree hoping he could quickly head back to the monastery and safety... but the giant's dog pursued him. And before long, the giant on horseback was beneath the trees following along as Jonah slowly climbed the treetops toward the monastery.

The giant's dog kept barking ruthlessly. Jonah could see the full size and figure of the giant just below him. He was a frightening creature. Jonah was terrified and soon began to panic. He also worried that the giant might shoot arrows up into the trees, as Jonah recalled the arrow that had struck Brother Thomas in the leg. Jonah panicked. He felt his muscles tighten and a surge of adrenaline, as he began to race along the branches. In his rush, he climbed onto a branch that could not support his weight. *CRAAAACK...* The branch broke and once again Jonah was falling! He remembered Rabbi Mortichai's words just before he left the monastery, *No lifeguard on duty.* As he tumbled, Jonah grabbed another branch, but his grip slipped and down he went. He fell, and fell, hitting and breaking branches. As he plunged downward you could hear the crackle of snapping branches. Eventually, Jonah hit the ground. He hit it hard... very hard.

The giant was soon there, and looking down from his horse he could see Jonah was motionless. The giant jumped down from his horse and checked Jonah for signs of life. Jonah was not breathing. The fall knocked the life out of him. After a silent moment, the giant lifted Jonah's lifeless body onto his horse and rode back to the maze and his house.

The giant entered the house carrying Jonah's limp body with him.

A girl was standing inside. Seeing the motionless lad, she shuddered with fear and gasped. "What did you do to him?" she quickly asked, and half afraid to hear the answer.

"Nothing, I've done nothing to him," the giant answered. "The fool panicked and fell from the trees," as he placed Jonah on a carpet near the wall.

"Is he dead?" the girl asked in a quivering voice.

"I think so," as he felt for a pulse in Jonah's wrist and then neck. "No pulse, and not breathing for some time now," shaking his head, "yes, this one's dead."

The trembling girl asked, "Why is he in the house?"

The giant didn't answer, but turned away and pulled a feather from his chest. He put the feather in the palm of Jonah's hand, and closed the lad's fingers around it.

"My feathers have some powers, yet there is no guarantee. No one is at fault here, but the final judge of innocence is left to Providence," as he pointed up for heaven's help.

CHAPTER 21

A GHASTLY SURPRISE

EARLY THE NEXT MORNING the girl woke before the giant. She walked over to Jonah, and leaned over to get a closer look at him. Just then, to her great surprise, Jonah opened one eye, and then the other. He had a frightening blank stare, like there was nothing behind his eyes. The girl was stunned, her jaw dropped and she fainted on the spot collapsing to the floor next to Jonah.

Slowly, Jonah sat up, looked around and saw the girl on the floor next to him. Now it was he who leaned over to get a closer look at her. But Jonah's vision was blurry and his thinking was muddled, yet he wondered, *Who is she? Is she sleeping?* While looking curiously at her, he heard someone snoring across the room. Although his vision was poor, he could see a large figure asleep on a bed. Instinctively, Jonah tried to stand and staggered toward the door. But Jonah was dizzy and weak, and soon stumbled, knocking some cups and plates off the table near him. The giant woke. His eyes scanned the room and quickly spotted Jonah struggling to remain standing. He got out of bed and stood.

"So, you're alive! Thank heavens! You don't know how lucky you are. Calm down," he told Jonah. "You can't leave anyway. The door is locked."

He could see the terror in Jonah's eyes, just before they closed again. Jonah passed out, and fell down landing right besides the girl.

The giant stood over his two unconscious prisoners and just stared before finally deciding to go outside and work. "In good time they will be fine, and he will work in my vineyard too."

Many hours later, Jonah's eyes flickered for a moment and then opened. His vision was slowly returning, and his ability to think clearly started to return. He looked up at a blank ceiling and wondered where he was. Then the face of a lovely young lady with long flowing brown hair appeared over his. She was looking straight into his eyes. She put a cool wet cloth on his forehead. Jonah looked into her soft eyes and thought, *am I dreaming?* After a few minutes, he was more alert and his vision fully cleared. As Jonah scanned the room's walls, he was shocked. Jonah knew the round walls meant he was inside the giant's round house at the center of the maze.

Suddenly, a large figure approached from behind the girl. It was the giant. He came chillingly close to Jonah. Jonah could feel his heart start to hammer. Then the giant spoke.

"You look better now," leaning over Jonah, "good skin color too." The giant asked, "Can you move your arms?"

Jonah slowly nodded and only slightly lifted both arms.

"Can you stand up?" the giant questioned.

Jonah slowly sat up, winced a little and rubbed his head. It was all he could mentally and physically do. But after a few moments, he knelt on the carpet with one knee and put one foot down on the floor. Then using his arms for support, he gradually stood up.

Now toe-to-toe with the giant, Jonah clearly saw the giant was tall, broad and mostly covered with small gray feathers. Jonah raised his head up, and got a good look at the giant's feathery face. The giant was colorless and ghostly with gray feathers and steely gray eyes. The pupils of his eyes were keyhole-shaped, as if some secrets were locked deep inside. He had one long eyetooth hanging down, as curled and twisted as a corkscrew. The strange sight shot fear through young

Jonah. Thunderstruck and bewildered, Jonah's legs weakened, he fell back onto the carpet, and sat there just staring up at the giant.

"Who are you and why are you in my vineyard?" the giant asked firmly.

Jonah was numb with shock, too frightened to answer, and just sat there silently on the carpet.

"Did you come for the girl?" he asked Jonah.

Jonah looked terrified, but the giant waited for an answer. Jonah's gaze located the girl. Finally, he was able to part his lips enough to weakly reply.

"No... uh... ummm... her? Who is she?" He stammered.

"Then why are you here?" demanded the giant now sounding hostile.

Nervous and still weak, Jonah tried to explain. But his words just tumbled out and he rambled on about how this all started with the King's contest.

"You see... there was this wild horse... and a contest... so I kept nagging and they called me an echo... then," shaking his head, "this rotten sunny day, so I went to church and prayed for clouds because, you know, the shadows... I was worried, but Father Croce talked to me." Jonah smiled, "and I did win... then I rode home on my new horse... but the next day a messenger came..."

The giant looked frustrated and irritated by Jonah's muddled answer.

"Stop!" ordered the giant holding up both hands. "Nonsense! You're talking gibberish. You must have hurt your head when you fell. Listen, you have not told me why you are here. What brings you to me? Is your brain ok?!"

Jonah, looking down at the floor collected his thoughts and managed to weakly answer. "Your feathers. I want a feather for King Leo." Jonah thought his answer sounded as strange as it was true.

Now the giant was more baffled than when he listened to Jonah's rambling about the King's contest, echoes, clouds and shadows. The giant wondered how anyone could know the power of his feathers. He thought, *If someone wants a feather, they must know its power.*

"Why? Why do you want my feather?" the giant pressed, wanting to know what Jonah knew.

Jonah, after a minute, calmed down further and was able to explain in a shaky voice.

"The King has been sick and is getting worse. His doctors fear he will soon die. But one doctor learned of a cure from a sorcerer's rhyme. And according to the rhyme, a feather from the giant will cure the King. So the King's doctor sent me here to find a feather in your vineyard. And there is a monk, Brother Thomas, who watches you from the treetops, he told me how to get here, and what your feathers look like."

The giant rubbing his head turned away wondering. *Who is this sorcerer, and how does he know about my feathers and their powers. Was he the one who cursed me and turned my body into this feathery monster?* The giant spun back around, and looked straight into Jonah's eyes.

"You cannot have even one of my feathers!" he shouted angrily. His voice seemed to bellow like thunder.

Frightened, Jonah scrambled to his feet, stood up again and suggested, "Ok, I guess I should go now and tell the King's doctor that you would not give me a feather."

Without lifting his eyes, Jonah started slowly walking backwards toward the door. "Anyway, I have to check on my horse, and also visit Father Croce and his cat that we need to feed, so I probably should leave now, and also... "

The giant interrupted Jonah's clumsy and weak excuses, and sternly replied, "Go? Go? Sit down! You think you can raid my vineyard to steal my feather and then just go? No, No, No! You're a raider, a trespasser, and will have to work for me in the vineyard, until the day I say you can go."

Jonah looked around, and seeing no windows and a large wooden door that was locked tight, saw no possible escape. He sat down again on the carpet.

"Look young fellow," said the giant as he pointed to the girl, "Julia has been here a few days. I found her wondering around in my maze. She got herself lost in the woods, and ended up in my maze while searching for wild berries to pick. Julia has been helping me with meals and other chores in the vineyard, and you will be a welcome addition to my new crew."

Jonah thought, *Julia? Could this be the same Julia that the monastery caretaker had mentioned from behind his closed bedroom door?*

The giant interrupted Jonah's thoughts, "What's your name?"

Jonah just stared for a moment, but then answered, "Jonah… ahh…ahh… Jonah Paladin."

"Ok then, nice to meet you, Jonah… ahh… ahh… Jonah Paladin," the giant teased. "Come, get up and sit here at the table."

Jonah stood up, walked over to the table and carefully lowered himself into the chair.

The giant pushed a large metal spoon and bowl toward Jonah. Jonah grimaced and squirmed a little in his chair, not knowing what was in the bowl.

"Here Jonah, Julia made rabbit stew for dinner. Have some. Tomorrow is a working day and you will need your strength."

The stew looked very dark and a bit strange. Cautiously, Jonah picked up the big spoon. But before he dipped it into the stew, he could see the giant's reflection in the spoon's shinny metal surface. Jonah saw the giant raise his upper lip and snarl, flashing his long corkscrew tooth. With his eyes still fixed on the spoon's reflection, Jonah then saw the giant's heavy arm suddenly reach towards him. In a rush of fear, Jonah dropped the spoon, cringed and quickly pushed his chair back away from the table.

The giant, with his long arm outstretched, grabbed a bottle of wine on the table near Jonah.

Instantly, Jonah realized the giant was not reaching for him, but instead the bottle. He exhaled and sighed with relief.

The giant raised the wine bottle to his mouth and pushed the cork against his strange corkscrew tooth. He turned the bottle a few times driving his tooth into the cork, and then pulled out the cork. The giant tore the cork from his twisted tooth and then poured half the bottle of wine into his mouth, swallowing it down in just a few loud gulps.

Jonah just stared and watched.

"Don't just stare at me Jonah, go ahead, eat the stew," the giant ordered.

Jonah obeyed and tasted the stew. "Not that bad. Tastes better than it looks." He nodded at Julia.

Julia frowned at him.

As Jonah ate, the giant checked the front door lock, and then locked a chain of bells across the doorway, which would alert him should anyone try to fiddle with the door. He muttered, "There, now the door is secure."

He turned to face Jonah, and pointed at a small bed next to the giant's large one. "Jonah, I made this bed for Julia, I'll make one for you too, but not until I trust you more. For now, you'll have to sleep under my bed so I know where you are." He threw a pillow and several empty burlap sacks under his bed for Jonah to sleep on.

Weary from the troubles of the day, they all quickly fell asleep and dreamed away.

CHAPTER 22
THE RIGHT "KEY" FOR A VIOLIN

DAYS PASSED. Jonah and Julia felt the throbbing of long days and nights. By day, they worked in the vineyard maze. And each evening they returned to the giant's dreary house for a meal and then retired early to bed. But one night after working in the vineyard, the giant surprised them when he opened a box and lifted out a violin. He then sat in a chair and began to play a few notes.

It was a good instrument but the strings were very much out of tune. And the giant couldn't play very well, so the sounds from the violin were truly awful. As the giant played he glanced over at Jonah and Julia for their reaction and encouragement. They both smiled and approvingly nodded their heads in unison, while they gritted their teeth. The horrid sounds screeched through the air. Even the mice dashed into their holes and right out of the house.

After some time Jonah interrupted the dreadful playing. "Sir, the music is fine, but the violin can use some tuning. If you allow me the opportunity, I should be able to fix up and tune your violin."

The giant stopped playing and pointed his violin bow at Jonah. "You? You're joking? What could you know about music?"

"My uncle repairs violins, and I've worked with him during summers."

The giant thought for a moment. "Ok, let's see what you can do with it."

The giant handed the violin to Jonah, who looked at it closely and said, "Your tuning pegs are stiff and not working right. Do you have a key that I can use to help make an adjustment?"

The giant looked at him suspiciously. "Hmmm... a key you say? What does a key have to do with tuning a violin?"

"Well, in my uncle's shop we used a key for leverage to help adjust a violin's stiff tuning pegs." Jonah pointed to the tight tuning pegs on the violin.

"Really? Jonah, that doesn't make any sense." The giant laughed. "Your uncle is wound-up too tight himself."

Jonah countered. "Sir, but I also learned the same technique in school when we studied musical notation and practiced on a violin… a violin from Cremona."

The giant looked surprised, and almost amused. "You went to school? Played a violin from Cremona? Look at you, you're just a jumble of tatters, don't make me laugh," as the giant eyed Jonah's shabby clothing.

"But it's true. I attended the Studium Generale collegium on the coast, and had money for the school, but not enough for a proper wardrobe."

The giant nodded. "Well, that would have been a good choice. Beauty is fleeting but knowledge is forever. Look at me, I am hideous but my mind is with me still… although trapped in this monster. But enough of that, I still don't believe you, you're a beggar or useless drifter at best."

Jonah explained. "Poor at birth, yes, but I'm not a drifter. I was fortunate to attend the collegium, and I can demonstrate proof of my education and schooling."

The giant laughed. "You have proof? Where is it?"

"Sir, allow me to describe the Fibonacci mathematical sequence, and how it's often displayed in nature and the universe."

The giant arched an eyebrow in disbelief. "You know about violins *and* can explain mathematics too?

Ok, this will be amusing, tell me something you know about Fibonacci," as he sat back in his chair.

Jonah then proceeded to provide a full review of the Fibonacci formulas, and even pointed out a few nearby examples. He explained, "A flower's seed and petal patterns often follow this mathematical formula, and so do the spiral seed patterns in the sunflowers here in your garden. This mathematical ratio is common throughout nature, and is also expressed in nautilus seashells, and even in the human body. For example, the bones in our fingers and hand contain this ratio." Jonah held out his left index finger, and with his right hand pointed to each finger bone, and then finally touched his left hand bone saying, "These four bones have the following proportions... 2, 3, 5, and 8. This is common design ratio that's functional, familiar and beautiful to our mind's eye. The ratio also exists in astronomy, and when applied in architecture, it's called *the golden ratio*. The Fibonacci mathematical sequence shows that throughout the universe there is a shared fundamental denominator that governs much design and creation."

The giant looked surprised as his eyes drilled at Jonah. "How did you do that?"

"Sir, I learned it when I attended the Studium Generale collegium."

The giant paused. "Well, I may have been mistaken about you. You might have attended the school, no vagrant could have explained all of that, and in such detail."

Then the giant thought for a moment, looked at his violin and nodded. "Ok, I'll get you a key," but he ordered, "turn around, and close your eyes. You too Julia."

The two followed the giant's instructions.

The giant walked over to the front door. He picked up his heavy hobnailed boot and lifted out the large key for the front door lock. He dropped the big boot to the floor, which made a loud thud that both Jonah and Julia heard.

While stealing a quick look at each other, Jonah and Julia had the same thought… *that thud sounded like the giant's boot dropping by the door.*

"Ok, you two can turn back around," as the giant stretched out his arm to hand Jonah the key.

Jonah pressed the key against the tuning pegs for leverage as he tightened and loosened the violin's tuning pegs and strings. The violin sounded better as Jonah plucked and tested the strings.

The giant grinned.

Jonah finished his adjustments and returned the key to the giant. He then asked the giant, "Would you have a smaller key that provides reduced leverage for finer adjustments?"

The giant, happy his violin was being improved, quickly replied, "Ok, but turn around and close your eyes again."

The two obeyed and turned their backs to the giant. But a moment later, Julia shook her head to swing her long hair, and managed to quickly peek between her flowing hairs at the giant. The giant was turned sideways, and Julia glimpsed as he dug through the feathers on his chest for the small key.

With the small key in his hand, the giant said, "Ok now, here Jonah, turn back around."

Jonah turned to face the giant who handed him a small key. It was the key for the small lock that secured the chain of bells across the door each night.

Jonah used the key to help make finer adjustments to the violin. When Jonah finished, he handed the small key and the violin to the giant, who turned his back to them and swiftly tucked the key under his chest feathers again. The giant then lifted the violin under his chin and plucked all of the stings. It now sounded much more like a tuned violin. But the giant barely knew how to play and the music was still unpleasant. Julia and Jonah kept frozen smiles on their faces, while hoping the playing would stop soon. But the giant was happily grinning and kept on playing.

Jonah and Julia kept nodding and smiling even though the giant's playing sounded like squealing pigs trying to sing. Jonah quietly mumbled to Julia, "It's best to just nod and smile… let the giant go on grinning."

Julia nodded to Jonah with a smile securely fixed to her face.

The giant played on and on into the night, but as it got late, he became drowsy and finally put the violin back in its box. "That was great, thank you Jonah, but it's late and we need to get some sleep."

The dreadful music thankfully stopped, and into bed they all finally flopped.

CHAPTER 23

QUICK THINKING
AND SLIGHT-OF-HAND

THE GIANT was now fast asleep. Jonah, under the giant's bed was wide-awake. The room's faint candlelight sparkled dimly in his eyes. Julia kept her eyes closed as they both listened to the giant snore for some time.

Jonah urgently whispered, "Julia, I think the large key to the door is in his boot."

She nodded in agreement as she softly slipped out of bed and tiptoed over to the giant's old, very smelly, big boot. The putrid boot stunk like rotting fish heads. Julia held her nose with one hand, and with her free hand felt around inside the repulsive boot. And there it was… she felt the key, and lifted it out. Then Julia silently returned to her bed and sat down. She cautiously leaned over and lifted a few of the giant's chest feathers. She started her search for the small key to unlock the chain of bells. Slowly, Julia pulled back feathers and gently felt for the key.

The giant began to stir. His head turned and the giant faced her.

Julia froze her finger in place and waited. After the giant's big bulbous nose blasted out another snore, she resumed her gentle search under his feathers. At last, up came her hand with the tiny key.

Julia took the small key and unlocked the chain of bells, then slowly and carefully placed it on the table. Next she gently unlocked the door. Then, like a bird balanced on a wire, Julia cautiously approached the sleeping giant once more. She sat on her bed again and reached toward him.

Looking fearful, Jonah wondered what she was doing. She already had both keys needed for their escape, and the front door was now unlocked. He was about to whisper a question. But before he could ask, Julia grabbed a feather, closed her eyes and gave a quick pull!

Jonah felt a jolt of fear. *What is she doing?*

Instantly, the giant opened an eye, then the other.

Julia froze as she clutched the feather in her hand. She closed her eyes.

The giant's gaze landed directly on Julia. He muttered, "What the devil are you doing?"

Still sitting up on her bed, Julia kept her eyes closed and explained softly, "I'm sorry, I was dreaming about picking grapes in the vineyard. I was asleep and must have pulled on your feather during my dream." She kept the feather concealed in the palm of her hand, and lay back down on the bed. With her eyes still closed she added, "Sorry, I'm so sleepy, it won't happen again."

The giant was groggy but awake enough to extend an arm. "The feather," he demanded with an open hand.

Julia opened an eye and was about to hand it over.

In a flash, Jonah was struck with an idea. He swiftly reached into his shirt and pulled out the sparrow's feather that he had found while traveling to the monastery and kept for good luck. Since Jonah was lying under the giant's bed, he easily lifted his feather into Julia's reach. She spotted Jonah's hand holding the feather, and knew exactly what to do. Julia gripped Jonah's bird feather between two fingers and passed it to the giant while her thumb kept the giant's feather hidden in her palm.

The drowsy giant didn't notice the sleight-of-hand, since a lone candle dimly lit the room. The giant stuffed the bird feather among his own, and was soon snoring loudly and out like a stone.

CHAPTER 24

WHICH WAY OUT?

NOW WITH THE DOOR unlocked and feather in hand, Jonah and Julia quietly slipped out of the house like thieves in the night. Under the soft moonlight they raced into the maze, but then suddenly stopped at the first intersection. Looking at each other they asked in unison.

"Which way out?" "What?"

Jonah burst out, "Since you've been here longer than me, I thought you had a plan to get us through the maze."

Julia snapped back, "Since you've worked in the maze more, while I mostly cooked, I thought you figured out how to get through."

Jonah shook his head. "We'll just have to climb over the vine-covered fencing and head toward the forest as fast as we can."

The two started climbing over the fencing.

Several moments passed.

Back at the house, the giant, a little itchy from the spot where his feather was plucked, began to scratch. He scratched and scratched until... one eye opened, then the other. The giant was awake. Now seeing the girl was gone, he quickly reached under his bed, and discovered Jonah was gone too. He thought, *Does that young fellow think he's playing Steal-the-Bride? Fine. I can play the bride's father. And here I come after you two!* Like an angry bear storming from his cave, the giant quickly rushed outside his house. He grabbed two nets, mounted his horse and galloped into the maze. He soon spotted the two climbing the vineyard fencing.

Jonah and Julia now heard the horse and saw the giant charging toward them!

"Listen, Julia, we can't keep climbing the fences, he can see us too easily. Let's split up and run through the maze in different directions, so at least one of us may get out of the maze and get help."

Julia nodded, and they dashed off in different directions in the maze. But suddenly, and to their surprise, they saw the giant riding back to his house. They wondered if their splitting up might have caused the giant to give up on catching them.

And so, the two kept running in opposite directions, or so they thought. They didn't realize that the twisting paths of the maze were turning them toward each other. As they both quickly turned a corner, they banged right into each other! Jonah and Julia both screamed at once and fell backwards onto the ground. Startled by the collision, they looked at each other with equal surprise, but quickly scrambled to get back up on their feet. And then in a flash, things got much worse. As they stood there, the two heard the frightening sound of a large dog barking loudly. To their dismay and disbelief, they quickly realized that the giant had returned to his house to let out his hunting dog to help him track down the pair of runaways.

Panic stricken, Jonah and Julia looked at each other desperate for any suggestion on what to do next.

Jonah offered, "Julia, here's a thought," and then screamed, "Run!"

Quickly, the two raced off again in opposite directions, hoping to somehow escape. But before they got very far the dog was on their heels. First caught was Jonah whose pants leg was being held tightly between the dog's snarling sharp teeth. Jonah struggled to get free before the giant got to him, but soon realized it was too late. Jonah soon heard the giant's horse just around the turn. Suddenly, the giant appeared on horseback, flung his net while still mounted, and quickly netted Jonah, who uttered only a grim sigh.

The giant jumped down from his horse and tied the net tightly around Jonah with rope. Jonah was once again heaped over the horse's back.

The giant leaped back onto his horse and raced toward Julia who was already trapped and cornered in the maze by the fierce barking dog. Soon the giant reached Julia and slid down from his saddle. She tried to speak, but before she could say anything, he flung a net over her, tied it, and also lifted her onto the horse next to Jonah. And back to the house they all went.

At the house, the giant carried each of his prisoners inside. Then he untied them, and immediately demanded his missing keys.

Julia stood there silently clutching the keys in her pocket.

The giant glared. "The keys," he repeated in a rough voice.

Julia gave just one long blink, and knew she had to surrender the keys. She extender her open hand and held out the keys.

The giant swung his arm toward her, and angrily snatched the keys from Julia's hand.

Julia's eyes slowly closed as she heaved a helpless sigh of despair, knowing there would be no second chance to get the keys again. She knew the giant would now make sure of that.

Jonah watched and gave her a weary look.

Then the giant locked his prisoners inside the house and slept just outside the door.

That night, the two prisoners barely slept, and even the giant had a twitchy, fidgety rest… at best.

CHAPTER 25

A BROTHER'S BROTHER?

THE NEXT DAY the giant sent Jonah and Julia to work in the maze to harvest grapes again. The giant was pruning a distant vine, but still kept a steady eye on them. As the two prisoners worked among the grapevines, they also looked for a feather. Although Julia already had one, looking for another helped pass the time. And they reasoned that two feathers would be better than one.

While working, Jonah and Julia also had some time and opportunity to talk as well. Julia, still troubled and mystified by the feather that brought Jonah back to life, finally had a chance to talk about it. But when she finished explaining what she had witnessed, Jonah wasn't convinced.

Jonah chuckled, "You're not serious. I was dead? It was some kind of trick the giant played on you, I'm sure."

Julia glared at him. "No! I really don't think so. Anyway, Jonah, aren't you here for a feather to cure the King? You've been told these feathers have powers."

Jonah partially agreed. "True, but curing an illness is a little different than bringing the dead back to life." Jonah made a deep spooky moan and wriggled his fingers around to tease Julia.

Julia was firm, and sternly answered, "Jonah, I saw what I saw, and you were dead. Dead as a doornail. Dead as yesterday. Dead as a herring in a fishmonger's basket."

"Ok, ok, I get it, Julia, you really think I was dead." Jonah didn't say anything else, but looked away and returned to picking grapes. He was quiet in his thoughts and not sure what to believe.

The next day, the two prisoners worked in the maze again. And again they looked for a feather, but still found none.

Jonah joked, "I really want to ask the giant... You look like a big bird, why don't you lose a feather once in a while like all the other creatures with feathers on the planet do? You have more gosh-darn feathers than a hundred birds, but we can't find one!"

Julia laughed while shaking her head.

The two kept on working... and hours passed.

Now the giant was close as he pruned a vine right next to them.

Jonah stopped working. He turned to the giant and was poised to say something.

Julia wondered what Jonah was up to.

Jonah asked, "Sir, how long do you plan on keeping us here?"

The giant kept on working, and didn't look at Jonah or answer.

Jonah continued, "The King will die soon if we don't bring him a feather, and Julia's father stays up all night at the monastery worrying about his missing daughter."

The giant ignored Jonah and instead turned to Julia asking, "So what you told me is true? You live in the monastery?"

Julia answered, "Yes, I told you the truth, I live in the monastery," as she glanced back at him.

The giant came closer. "Julia, so do you know Brother Thomas, the monk who lives there too?"

Julia was surprised that the giant knew the monk's name, and answered, "Yes, of course, I know Brother Thomas very well. My father is the monastery caretaker and works for Brother Thomas. I guess you've seen the monk as he sometimes watched you from his tree-top nest?"

"Yes, I've seen him. Well, actually, I knew someone had regularly spied on me for the last year, but rarely comes now."

Jonah thought, *The giant must not know that one of his arrows struck the monk in the leg, which is why he rarely comes now.*

The giant continued, "I was pretty sure it was the monk, but at times I thought it was his friend the rabbi up there in the trees. The rabbi and the monk are close friends. I'm surprised the two weren't up there spying on me together with their creepy little eyes peeking out from that ridiculous nest. And they think I'm strange," he chuckled. "Once I shot arrows at his nest to chase him away, but I may have scared him more than I had intended. One arrow almost hit him right in the head! I didn't want him hurt, just gone. And I didn't know for certain that it was the monk up there, but it looked like him."

Julia trying to learn more asked, "So, Sir, you know the rabbi too?"

"Yes, I know him and many people who live in the village," he replied.

Julia and Jonah both looked surprised.

Then Jonah felt compelled to ask, "So, how is it that you know the monk, and why is he so curious about what you do out here?" It was a question Jonah had asked Dr. Sano and the monastery caretaker too, but was never answered.

The giant just stared back silently, but after a long pause gave an answer that shocked both Julia and Jonah.

"The monk is my brother."

"Brother?!" thought Julia and Jonah. Their surprise was clear, as they stood in stunned silence.

Jonah thought and then asked, "Do you mean the monk is... a Brother? You know, a religious Brother? Since he is a monk, we call him by the title of Brother, is that what you mean?"

"No," the giant said firmly, "the monk is my younger brother. I was born a man like him. We are brothers." The giant continued, "Some kind of curse turned me into this feathery creature. At first, I thought my brother, Thomas, became a monk and joined the monastery to pray for me after I became this feathery monster. But then I started to think that he became a monk because of some guilt he had, and that somehow he was responsible for this evil curse cast upon me. I'm not sure why he spied on me, but it might be due to his guilt."

Trying to convince the giant to set them free Jonah continued, "The King sent me to your own brother, Brother Thomas, so that I would learn from him how to climb through the forest and find a feather here in your vineyard. Thomas knows I am here, and if you keep us prisoners your brother will think you're a criminal... and so will the King."

"That is if the King lives," the giant snapped back in a rough tone. "And let them both think whatever they choose," the giant said without any apparent emotion or concern.

Jonah replied, "Your brother and the entire town will hate you if the King dies. And the King's sons are both missing, so if he dies there will be a war among the knights for power. That will be our fate."

"Fate? Fate?" scowled the giant. "Fate turned me into this monstrous state."

CHAPTER 26
CREATIVE LOGIC

THE GIANT WAS SILENT for some moments lost in thought, but then announced, "Fate, yes *fate*, should decide what I do with you two bothersome trespassers. I have an idea."

The giant looked around in the vineyard at the bushels and sacks of grapes. He then reached into a bushel and picked up a plump, round grape. "Let's play a game to decide your fate," the giant declared.

He then also picked up a flat, squashed grape from the ground. He showed the two grapes to Jonah and Julia. "I'll drop these two grapes into an empty sack, and you can pick one out. If you pick the round grape,

I will let you free. But if you pick the squashed grape, you must agree to stay, and not try to escape any more."

As the giant raised his closed hand that held the two grapes over the sack, all eyes were firmly focused. But when he opened his hand to let the grapes fall into the sack, Julia noticed drops of grape juice fall from the giant's hand as well. She clearly saw the drops as they glistened in the sunlight. Julia quickly realized, *the giant squashed the round grape before dropping it into the sack. The sack contains **two** squashed grapes and **no** round one! The giant was cheating, there was no way to win!*

"Who shall pick and decide your fate?" asked the giant with a knowing smile.

They all stood silently and stared at the sack. A moment passed.

Then, Jonah and Julia both answered together, "I will."

"No, no, I will," insisted Julia, as she moved in front of Jonah to stop him from picking. Jonah tried to step in front again but she pulled him back. Julia was a very smart and logical person. Now facing trouble, her logical mind found an ingenious solution to the problem, so she wanted to pick the grape herself. Before Jonah could move again, Julia swiftly reached into the sack.

The giant smiled as he knew there were two squashed grapes in the sack, and Julia had no chance to pick a round grape and win freedom.

Inside the sack, Julia's hand closed around one of the two squashed grapes, as the giant had planned. But she kept her hand closed as she lifted it out of the sack. And just then, Julia sneezed unexpectedly, causing her to drop the grape on the ground. It was now lost among many other round and squashed grapes on the ground.

Julia apologized, "I'm very sorry, my sneeze made me drop the grape," as she showed the giant her empty hand. Then quickly she added, "So, we don't know which grape I picked from the sack since it dropped to the ground. But if we look at which grape *remains in the sack*, we can determine which grape I picked out and dropped. It's a simple process of elimination." Julia explained, "If the sack contains a squashed grape, that means I must have picked and dropped the round one, it's only logical."

Julia smiled as she enjoyed her logical solution, as well as the double pleasure of outwitting the cheating giant.

The giant looked startled and even a little puzzled.

Julia then quickly slipped her hand into the sack again, pulled out a squashed grape, and held it out for the giant to see. She announced, "You see, a squashed grape, which means that I must have picked out and dropped the round grape! So, *fate* will now set us free!"

The giant clearly was surprised by Julia's clever actions. But then his surprise turned to anger as the giant realized he was beaten by Julia's logic and intellect.

Suddenly, the giant waved his massive arm and shouted at them in a rough voice, "Forget it. Deal off. Get back to work!"

Julia was a girl whose temper had a long fuse, but when fully burned, a fiery rage erupted. As she stood facing the giant she was appalled at first, then angry, and gradually grew furious. Her eyes glared back at him from being cheated, and her face turned crimson. Feeling now there was nothing to lose she slammed back, "You're a liar, a two-faced liar!"

At this impasse and low point, Jonah knew there was no way to salvage the current situation. And his playful mind flashed and found humor in their dilemma. Standing near Julia, he grinned and looked a bit mischievous. He winked at her and whispered a little joke that came to his mind. He smiled. "Honestly, Julia, if the giant had two faces would he be wearing that ugly feathery one?"

Jonah whispered his joke for Julia to hear and enjoy… but so did the giant!

The giant breathed in deeply and his chest swelled out.

Jonah winced in regret, realizing that the giant had heard him. He wished that he could somehow drop through the earth where he stood and simply disappear.

The giant scowled at him and blasted, "What did you say about my face? Do you think you're funny? Maybe I should tie you to the fence and leave you for the wolves tonight!"

The expression on Jonah's face swiftly changed, and his eyes widened with fright.

Then the giant folded his arms across his chest. His scowl deepened and he shrouded himself in silence.

Julia and Jonah stood silently not sure what was next.

Curiously, the slightest hint of a grin seemed to cross the giant's lips. Then he smiled and a moment later he erupted into laughter.

Jonah and Julia looked at each other and didn't know what to make of it.

Then the giant laughed louder and harder, and was laughing like a madman. It was a frightening laugh, one that could scare the green right off of grass. Then suddenly and surprisingly the giant stopped laughing altogether. The giant stood silently again, and looked lost in his thoughts.

Jonah wondered, *What thoughts could be swirling inside the silent process of the giant's brain, covered by a mysterious mound of feathers. What is he thinking, what will this silent creature choose to do next?*

Humor can feel like ridicule, but sometimes it is disarming, lightens the mood and brings agreement. Luckily, this time Jonah's little joke was disarming, and the giant was able to see the humor in Jonah's words. The subdued giant began to smile again.

Then shaking his head, the giant chuckled and his tone softened. "Ha ha, I haven't laughed that hard in a very long time. Jonah, your little quip really is kind of funny. In fact, I did once have another face, a more human face. And believe it or not, inside of me, I am actually more human than monster."

Now the giant faced Julia. "Ok Julia, you have won fairly, and you are too clever to keep imprisoned anyway. Also, my vineyard maze was built to keep people *out*... it was not built to keep people *in*. It's time for you to go. But I am grateful for having you two with me these past days... grateful for your work and companionship. I once heard that a home is like an opera, both need a story and voices. And your voices have turned my lonesome shelter into a home."

The giant turned away and motioned to them, "You two, follow me." The giant began to walk through the vineyard maze toward his house.

Jonah and Julia looked uncertain. They still couldn't believe their ears, but followed along.

The giant took them behind the house where there was as a wagon. He then hitched his horse to it.

"Get in, let's go, I'll take you both out of here," the giant announced calmly.

Although suspicious, they had no choice and climbed into the wagon hoping for the best. The two were unsure of the giant's behavior, half-expecting a trap and not a favor.

CHAPTER 27

FREEDOM FOR TWO, BUT NEW TROUBLES BREW

J ONAH AND JULIA RODE with the giant through the maze, then out into the forest and toward freedom. As the group traveled deeper into the forest, Nico and Pico spotted them. The two little squirrels dashed toward the wagon and jumped, unnoticed, onto the rear axle to travel along. But as they rode through the forest something was happening. There were sinister faces... foul, angry faces, appeared on the trunks of the forest trees they passed. No one noticed except for Nico and Pico who sat backwards on the axle watching these frightening faces appear. The squirrels looked at each other in puzzlement, and just shrugged their shoulders.

Finally, the group reached the clearing at the end of the forest.

"Go," the giant commanded. "And do not return, I may have a different heart in this matter if you do."

Jonah and Julia jumped down from the wagon and turned to leave.

"Wait," the giant said loudly. Then he pulled a feather from his chest, reached down from the wagon and handed it to Jonah. "This is for the King."

"Thank you," Jonah said looking more surprised than pleased by the generous gift. "We'll get this to King Leo today," he added.

"Goodbye," were the giant's last words, as he quickly spun his wagon around.

Jonah and Julia stood silently watching, as the giant raced back into the dense forest and disappeared forever from their sight.

Walking briskly, Jonah and Julia started their hike toward the monastery. It would be a long walk, but one that they welcomed. After walking and talking for some time, they spotted a willow tree, and decided to sit beneath it to take a short rest.

Jonah turned to face Julia. "I've been wondering about something."

"Wondering about what?" Julia happily chimed.

"Julia, remember the round and squashed grapes in the giant's game-of-fate."

Julia nodded and gently smiled.

"I was just wondering, when you sneezed and dropped the grape that you picked from the sack, was that planned or did you really sneeze and accidentally drop the grape?"

"Well, why do you care Jonah? We're free, and that's all that really matters now," Julia teased. Her lips were pressed together to restrain a smile, as she glanced at him playfully.

"True Julia, getting out of there was the important thing, but I still would like to know how the grape was dropped. It's a fair and logical question to ask. And Julia, you know about logic, right?" Jonah countered as he teased back at her.

"Yes Jonah, it is a fair and logical question. But before I answer your question about the grapes, can you tell me if your uncle really repairs violins? That's what you told the giant," Julia joked.

Jonah laughed. "But Julia, you answered my question with another question," shaking his head. "But ok, I'll answer you. Yes, my uncle did make repairs."

"Violin repairs?" Julia raised an eyebrow as she pressed on.

Jonah laughed again. "Well, the truth is, my uncle is a cobbler, but since his shop has lots of shoe leather, he once repaired a leather violin case." Jonah chuckle, "And that seemed close enough at the time." He tilted his head and grinned.

Julia laughed. "Agree, that certainly was close enough and just what we needed right then and there."

And so, the two resumed walking and kept talking, learning more about each other on their hike to the monastery. They talked and talked. And teased and taunted each other too. They were simply happy and immensely relieved to be free and on their way home. They had survived a lot together in the last few days. Jonah also told Julia about his adventures climbing through the forest. And he described Fayrissa and how she had sent two squirrels to help him. Jonah explained the squirrels could talk, and had told him that they were cousins too.

Julia laughed, "Cousins?"

Jonah nodded. "Yes, they were quite insistent on that."

Soon Julia held Jonah's hand. He glanced at her and smiled. He felt himself flush slightly. In time, arrows of mutual affection would pierce their hearts from a quiver with no limits.

CHAPTER 28

THE VALUE OF A GOOD DEED

Finally, Jonah and Julia reached the monastery. Julia's father, the caretaker, hugged her for a long time before either of them spoke. Jonah quickly hopped on Shadow and headed for the King's castle with the feather the giant had given him. He hoped he wasn't too late.

Jonah reached the castle gates, and was greeted by Dr. Sano. He hugged Jonah briefly and then hurried him straight to the King's bedroom.

They reached the bedroom door and Dr. Sano knocked. The door slowly opened and the Queen appeared. She gasped when she first saw Jonah standing there.

Jonah lifted his hand with the feather.

Queen Regina closed her eyes and hugged Jonah.

"Jonah, come in," she said excitedly. She took Jonah's hand and moved him close to the King's bedside.

"Are you awake, Leo," she mildly questioned.

The King's bright green eyes opened. His lips parted, but before he could speak, he instantly spotted Jonah.

"Jonah. It's you." He stared silently for a moment.

Jonah nodded and handed the feather to King Leo.

The King smiled warmly. He was thrilled to have the feather, and overjoyed to see that Jonah had returned completely unscathed. Inwardly, he was also pleased that he had correctly judged Jonah's ability to succeed.

The King examined the feather closely. "Jonah, I was certain that you would somehow succeed. So, how exactly did you manage this?"

Jonah smiled. He hesitated. He wasn't sure where to even start, so much had happened. But before he could answer, Dr. Sano caught the room's attention as he suddenly walked over to the window. He pointed to a horse-drawn wagon racing toward the castle.

"Who are they?" he asked, alarmed at their approaching speed.

Everyone in the room watched as the wagon with two men advanced toward them.

As it neared, Jonah recognized that it was the giant's horse and wagon. He thought, *Does the giant want his feather back?* Jonah felt a chill as he watched the wagon travel closer. Dark memories were too fresh.

Finally, it became clear who rode on the wagon. It was Brother Thomas the monk, along with another man that Jonah didn't recognize.

In a sudden burst of energy, the King rose up from his bed, stood and loudly called, "Our sons, Thomas and James!" He turned to the Queen and pointed out the window. "Regina, our two sons are finally back!"

Soon the King and Queen were embracing their two sons who were missing for a year. Their hearts soared. For the first time, in a very long time, the King's face glowed with contentment. He smiled broadly. No one was certain if it was the feather or the return of the sons to the family that helped the King, but his health appeared to immediately improve.

After the King embraced his sons, King Leo looked them over carefully. "Thankfully, you boys look quite well. But we've been sick to death with worry. Where have you two been? And Thomas, why are you wearing a monk's robe?" The King shook his head slightly, and looked a bit bewildered.

Thomas began to explain, and sounded near tears as he spoke. "Father, this is all my fault, I've made a terrible mistake that will pain me for the rest of my life. Where do I begin?" He paused. Then Thomas lowered his head and gently sobbed.

In the room, everyone stared in silence.

Finally, Thomas regained his composure. He lifted his head and continued. "My brother James was under a horrible curse that turned him into the creature known by many in Liguria... as the feathered giant."

Then Thomas embraced James tightly. "Thank you for forgiving me," he told his brother.

Everyone was startled and puzzled as they strained to understand what Thomas was just beginning to explain.

Thomas continued, his voice was heavy with emotion. "All this trouble started a year ago. I was jealous that my older brother, James, was heir to the King's thrown. In a fit of greed and jealously, I went to visit the sorcerer, Saggio, in the forest and paid him for witchcraft. I asked Saggio to help me become the crown's heir. So, the sorcerer cast a curse that turned James into a creature. James fled to the forest to hide his monstrous appearance from the townsfolk who would fear and persecute him."

Thomas shook his head and humbly continued. "I saw the evil curse strike my brother, James, and my greed and jealously soon turned to guilt and regret. Unbearable sorrow haunted my soul. My anguish and guilt drove me to join the monastery, and I became a monk to pray for James and be forgiven." He cleared his throat. "Deep in the forest, James built a window-less house surrounded by a vineyard maze to keep people away. But, I wanted to be near my brother and see him. So, I built a treetop nest in the forest so I could watch James, who was now trapped in the body of this feathery creature."

The stunned King was not sure which of his many questions to ask next, but then turned to his son James and said, "You're no longer a feathered giant, so what freed you from the sorcerer's evil spell?"

Dr. Sano stepped forward to explain. "The sorcerer's rhyme may help answer your question Sire." The doctor unfolded his notes, and recited part of Saggio's rhyme:

A prince was turned to a feathery breed,
But can break the spell with just one good deed.

Then Jonah explained further. "Yes, it was a good deed that broke the spell. It was broken by the giant's good deed. The giant, I mean James, set us free and also gave us a feather to heal the King. So, his good deed set us free, and in doing so set himself free from the spell as well. Just as the rhyme says it would."

After understanding what had happened and hearing the mournful confession from Thomas, the

King forgave him for the suffering that he had caused James.

King Leo declared, "Thomas your greed led you into trouble, and caused horrors for your brother. But we all make mistakes in life, and the truly big lessons of life are often learned the hard way. This was a hard lesson, but since your brother James has forgiven you, Thomas, then so too can your parents." He looked at the Queen who nodded her agreement.

The King stared Thomas in the eye. "Had this happened when I was a younger man, I would have sent you to prison, at least until the Queen could get you out. But much sand has emptied from the hourglass of my life, and so I can now see things more clearly. And my many years have nurtured a gentle tolerance, having learned that it is forgiveness that truly binds a family."

Queen Regina added, "Thomas, your actions caused terrible hardships. But these actions are past, and we forgive you now. The time is always right to do what is right, and forgiveness is what's right. It's important that the family is united in harmony... concordia. Every family must seek and nurture concordia."

As it grew late, they retired to their bedrooms and Jonah was invited to stay the night. However, with all the excitement of the day, Jonah couldn't sleep that night. Awake in bed with eyes open, Jonah came to realize the full value and power of that one single good deed, because it... freed himself and Julia... freed James from the spell that had turned him into a giant... saved the King's life... returned both sons, James and Thomas, to the family... and prevented a war among the knights for power.

Jonah learned that each good deed has hidden values that are not apparent, but these benefits ripple though the lives of many individuals who are helped by it.

Although Jonah's mind was still swirling with thoughts, he began to feel the tug of sleep, and his eyes became tired and heavy. And as he rested half-conscious Jonah had another striking realization. He thought... *it was not some process within the giant's **brain** that moved him to free Julia and me, and give us a feather to save the King's life. But rather, it was the giant's **heart** that led him to his good deed.* Jonah now knew that the dying King was the giant's father. That bond does not easily break... time nor tide cannot wear it away. And that night, just as his eyes closed tightly for sleep, Jonah learned an important lesson, *that the heart is the captain of the mind.*

Upstairs in the King's bedroom, the King sat awake in a chair gazing out a window at the distant forest.

Although ecstatic that he was reunited with his sons, the King sensed trouble. King Leo was worried about the sorcerer whose spell was broken by his son's good deed. The King recalled the last line of the sorcerer's rhyme.

Should this deed be done something happens
to me,
But no one knows what that would be.

As the King stared out from his bedroom window, he said to himself, "The rhyme says something unknown will happen to the sorcerer, and that must have Saggio very concerned and distressed. The only question now is… What is this unknown event that will happen to Saggio? I sense trouble brewing tonight." The King's instincts were right as rain, once again.

CHAPTER 29
THE BATTLE'S ECHO

T HAT NIGHT, the moon was like a big orange pumpkin hanging low near the horizon. Against the orange moon, silhouetted tree branches looked like some kind of sinister graffiti. Tonight, something strange and ominous was happening deep in the forest. Many of the forest's trees grew ugly menacing faces on their trunks. Some were horrible and ghastly, but others looked so peculiar they were a little comical.

Nico and Pico were running and hopping from tree to tree looking at these odd faces. They laughed at the funny faces and expressions, and made some of their own, as they copied and mimicked what they saw. They pulled their little squirrel mouths wide open with their paws, and stuck out and wiggled their tongues. Then they laughed still louder. Pico leaned close as he made a funny face at one of the tree faces. In a flash, the tree's face grew horribly frightful, and seemed to jump from the tree trunk right at him. Pico leaped backwards screaming and tumbled into Nico behind him. Nico had been watching it all and howled with laughter. But then they couldn't believe what happened next. Their eyes opened wider still as they watched entire tree trunks begin to shudder violently and then swell. Something very bizarre was happening, and it wouldn't end well.

The tree trunks and branches began to stir and change shape. Trunks twisted. Branches bent. Then leaves went flying in every direction as trees shuddered and trembled terribly. The trees started forming strange new shapes. Some began to look like four-legged creatures, while others seem to grow two legs instead. Then tree roots were pulled up, and dirt flew up into the sky. So much dirt flew into the sky that it blocked most of the moon from view. The forest became darker and darker as loads of dirt flew up into the air. As the flying dirt finally began to settle back to the ground, the details on these new creatures could now be seen.

Soon it was obvious that an entire forest was turning into wooden horses with wooden soldiers riding them. The soldiers had grayish tree bark for skin.

Their eyes were black wooden tree knots that seemed to stare blankly ahead, and with a gaze as emotionless as stones. When these soldiers turned their heads, their eyes never moved. The ghastly stare gave them a frightening appearance. Their horses had no fur at all, and were also covered in tree bark. And their fearsome horseheads had no eyes, perhaps the riders on their backs guided these wooden monsters.

Then these creatures began to move. They were walking, and then marching in neat rows. The soldiers on horseback were cavalry, and each soldier had one arm that was a long log with a pointed end. The massive arm could knock down several men with a single blow, and its pointed end could be rammed straight through any castle doors.

By morning, an entire wooden army began their advance... on the town! Rows and rows of mounted soldiers, all of wood, began their slow but steady procession to the King's castle. The town's "jewel-box" would soon be under attack. The people in the countryside were the first to see these threatening wooden warriors approaching. Many screamed as they fled into town for protection within the castle walls. They warned the townsfolk that a horrifying army was nearing.

The King's soldiers let the people in, and then lifted the castle's drawbridge to lock out the approaching army. Now the moat's deep water surrounded and protected the castle. But this protection soon became useless. When the army reached the moat, the wooden soldiers and horses easily floated across the moat's waterway. The King's men shot flaming arrows and hurled stones at the approaching soldiers. Some burned. Others were smashed to smithereens. But more wooden soldiers on horseback kept coming from the forest.

In the forest, Nico and Pico ran out from the hollow of Fayrissa's tree house carrying strong ropes, and headed for the battle. They strung these ropes across the path of the oncoming soldiers to trip their horses. And the squirrels danced around in full view to draw the army towards them and their traps. And Nico shouted rude names at them.

Nico yelled, "Hey, wood brains, termite food. Yes, I'm talking to you splinter rot," as he pointed at the soldiers. "Come and get us you wooden knot-heads. Come and fight, we'll turn you into firewood for roasting our acorns, and for warming our fuzzy little butts tonight."

Even Pico, who never spoke, laughed hard at that last insult. He thought, *Warming our fuzzy little butts tonight, that one is precious cousin Nico.*

Many of the wooden creatures marched toward the two squirrels and tripped, falling over, and could not get up. The squirrels repeated their trap many times and rolled with laughter as they watched the wooden army pile up and block others from marching toward the castle. Wooden creatures that got past these traps were set ablaze by the flaming arrows shot at them by the King's soldiers. As the smoke rose, people in the castle cheered. There was a feeling of renewed confidence that victory was near.

But their joy and rejoicing were short lived. More and more trees turned into soldiers and horses. A new wave of soldiers was forming and now approaching. There seemed to be no end to a long line of enemy combatants. Soon, the wooden warriors vastly outnumbered the King's men, and the beautiful "jewel-box" castle and town were clearly destined for destruction.

Jonah rode Shadow along the castle walls shooting flaming arrows at the wooden soldiers who were now scaling the walls. Jonah's horse, once afraid of its own shadow, was now riding with his trusted master in a fierce battle. Jonah rode hard, but could see the battle would soon be lost to this slow moving, but relentless army of wood. All hope was vanishing, just as a sand-castle is slowly washed away by the sea.

Then in a moment of desperation, Jonah remembered Fayrissa who had helped him before. He urgently needed to head to the forest and look for her. Jonah asked the King's archers for cover. They unleashed a hail of flaming arrows at the wooden soldiers near Jonah, so he could ride safely out of the castle.

The castle's drawbridge was just half lowered. Jonah approached it looking very determined. He swallowed hard, gave Shadow a firm pat, and together they charged over the drawbridge and leaped into the air. After soaring over the water below, they landed safely on the other side of the moat.

He and Shadow raced through the storm of the battle and towards the forest. Jonah's adrenalin surged and his heart pounded as hard as Shadow's hoofs struck the ground. He rode while dodging blows from the wooden soldiers that could kill a man. Luckily, Shadow's speed and agility easily out maneuvered the slower moving wooden army.

Jonah was hoping Fayrissa had returned from her trip to Duiblinn, and that he could quickly find her. But on his way to the forest, he suddenly remembered the monastery, which gave Jonah another idea. Jonah turned and raced toward the monastery. Moments later, he reached the building, but the monastery was sealed tight. Its doors were locked and windows shuttered because of the battle that was raging in the town. He began to circle it on horseback and called out to Julia.

"Julia, Julia, it's me, open a window."

No one answered.

Jonah kept calling for her.

Moments passed.

Finally, one shutter on a high window cracked opened. Then Julia peaked out, but looked anxious. "Come in, it's not safe out there, I'll open a small door in the back."

Hastily, Jonah shook his head and shouted back, "No time. Please listen. This is urgent. My mother once told me about a little girl who used to shout from the top of a tall monastery tower to create an echo off the nearby mountains. She said the girl could be heard for miles around. Have you heard about this story?"

"Yes," Julia answered with a knowing look.

"Julia, I need your help. Please, go up to the top of the tower and call to Fayrissa. We desperately need her help at the castle."

"Ok, I know what to do," she answered without hesitation. And Julia knew *exactly* what to do. She was the little girl in the story that Jonah had learned about from his mother.

Jonah rode off to try and find Fayrissa's tree house again.

Julia raced up the stairs to the top of the tower, and was standing higher than the forest treetops. She called out for Fayrissa to help the embattled town and castle. Julia's echoing calls for help bounced among the mountaintops, and then across the entire valley just as it did when she was a child.

In the forest, Fayrissa, who had just returned from her trip, was alarmed hearing Julia's clarion call for help. Fayrissa spun and looked around. Then she saw the smoke above the town, and knew there was trouble.

In a flash, Fayrissa soared up and over the forest. She immediately spotted the dreadful faces on tree trunks, and the strange wooden army marching towards the town. From her hands she threw gleaming lightning bolts in the shape of large ocean stingrays. These bright bolts of stingray-shaped lightning blasted the wooden army and trees. But as she flew past them, the army quickly resumed marching, and the faces quickly grew back on the tree trunks.

She flew through the forest and then to the castle, and shot her bolts at the battling wooden army. But these bolts did little to slow the army's tireless advances. Fayrissa's bolts were shaken off the wooden army like mere snowflakes from a dog's back. She began to realize that her powers were not strong enough to help, and something told her that Saggio was to blame... once again.

Flying above the castle, Fayrissa now looked over the enchanted forest and toward Saggio's hut. Her anger was unchained, and her face scowled. For a moment she looked more terrifying than the faces on the trees. Like a wild tornado, she soared back into the forest. On her way, she swooped down to grab Nico and Pico, who went along for the ride, but even they were frightened by the angry look on Fayrissa's face.

As she flew, all three could see more and more trees growing faces and limbs, and joining the marching army. She went deep into the forest, straight for the sorcerer's hut. Sitting on Fayrissa's shoulders, as she soared barely above the treetops, Nico and Pico bravely held on for dear life.

"Hang on cousin," Nico shouted.

Pico looked over, cringed and nodded.

CHAPTER 30

A HIDDEN NEGOTIATION

As Fayrissa and her two squirrels flew closer to the hut, the clever sorcerer sensed their approach. Fayrissa flew down to the hut with Nico and Pico still perched on each of her shoulders. She swiftly swept a few spiders off the hut's front door and knocked hard.

"We'll soon see how clever this sorcerer really is," she threatened.

Slowly the sorcerer appeared as he carefully opened the door.

Fayrissa quickly engaged him. "Saggio, what are you doing! Have you gone completely mad?!"

"Leave while you can, Fayrissa. This is not your fight," he warned anxiously.

"No! You've gone too far this time." Her bold stare hardened. "Stop this madness at once, or I'll be forced to join the others against you."

"Fayrissa, you have to understand. Listen to me. Someone has broken my spell with a good deed. Such an act creates a serious danger for me. I must win this battle, capture James, and turn him back into a feathery monster... or I will suffer from some unknown consequences. And I do not wish to find out what these consequences are the hard way. So, I'm warning you one last time, leave while you can."

Fayrissa stood her ground. Her bright blue topaz eyes glared with a crystal-clear message that she was not leaving.

Saggio looked unsure and hesitated, but finally pulled a two-headed fanged serpent from behind his back for her to see. He hoped to intimidate Fayrissa and frighten her away.

But Fayrissa fearlessly moved forward and began to enter the doorway. Her soft beauty was only surpassed by her steely courage.

Saggio looked tense and his jawbone tightened. A tide of conflicting emotions welled up within him. His long-time admiration and feelings for Fayrissa made him uneasy and waver. But in this desperate instant, Saggio's survival instincts surged and overwhelmed all other thoughts and feelings. Then in one quick move-ment, Saggio raised his arm high to heave the beastly snake at Fayrissa.

Seeing the danger, Nico and Pico swiftly jumped off Fayrissa's shoulders and right onto Saggio, as they clung tightly to his shirt. The poor sorcerer was shocked. He jumped and stumbled, but held onto the monstrous looking snake. Saggio staggered back-wards, and crashed into the fireplace kettle as his rear flopped right into it.

At the same time spiders flooded the room com-ing out of rainspouts, cracks, and up from between floorboards.

Nico and Pico tried to hold back Saggio's arm, but were quickly tangled by spider webs that were flung upon them by the numerous insects.

While still sitting in the fireplace kettle, Saggio quickly hurled the snake at Fayrissa standing in the doorway. The snake flew across the room and straight at her. Fayrissa was so busy pulling spider webs off her face and hair that she didn't see the two-headed snake flying towards her with both jaws open, and slimy fangs ready for its victim.

Suddenly, a rider on horseback swooped Fayrissa up and right out of the hut's doorway! She looked up. It was Jonah and Shadow! The snake missed Fayrissa and fell to the ground. Shadow kicked it into the woods.

Fayrissa looked up at Jonah and gave a quick, but thankful, slap on his chest. "I'll see you later, I still need to deal with Saggio." She leaped down from the horse and into the hut through an open window.

Inside the hut, she and Saggio's eyes immediately locked. But before Saggio could move, Fayrissa quickly cast her stingray-shaped lightning bolts that struck Saggio squarely in his chest. A blast of sparks flew around him as he was fiercely pushed backwards. Saggio gasped and then fell flat on his back. At first the sorcerer looked hurt, but in a flash he smiled and then suddenly wheeled back up onto his feet with a new surge of strength. Saggio swiftly moved toward Fayrissa, who was startled by his quick recovery and abrupt advance. Fayrissa hastily leaped backwards with her arms outstretched for balance.

"I did warn you Fayrissa," then Saggio cast a powerful spell, saying:

North to East, we see the least.
As day is day, she must stay.

Immediately Fayrissa was frozen and her skin was turned as white as milk. She was made motionless by the spell that Saggio quickly blurted out. Her eyes were frozen in an open stare, and Fayrissa couldn't even move an eyelash. She was like a beautiful marble statue with her slender arms outstretched.

"Now fair Fayrissa, you must stay and be mine forever," exclaimed Saggio happily, "and without your interference the battle will easily be won by my wooden cavalry. And James will be captured and turned back into a feathered giant, as he was before he broke my curse. My future is now safe and secure."

Jonah had just entered the hut in time to hear the spell and saw the horror of how it froze Fayrissa. He stood in stunned silence… she was his last and only hope. Inwardly, his head was spinning, uncertain what to do next. His heart sunk, as he knew all was lost.

Saggio approached Jonah and put his arm around Jonah's shoulders in a friendly way, as they both stared at Fayrissa.

"Jonah, for years I've had a special interest in her, well actually, more like admiration and affection. Fayrissa is beautiful and smart, brave and powerful. She is pretty much perfect for me. But of course she doesn't agree."

Jonah turned to look at Saggio. "If you feel for her, why not free her from your spell?"

"I'd like to free her, Jonah, but she will cause too much trouble for me, and the things I need to do. Jonah, you have to understand that the giant broke my spell with a good deed, and so I'll be subject to some consequences that are unknown. For my safety, I need to win today's battle, capture James and turn him back into the feathery creature. Fayrissa will fight me in every step. She just now almost killed me."

Jonah nodded slightly.

A few moments passed as they both gazed at Fayrissa.

"Jonah, I've been thinking, please sit with me at my desk. I'd like to show you something." Saggio walked over to his desk, Jonah followed, and the two sat down. On the desk was a wooden box with elaborate carvings on it. There were planets, stars and moons, as well as the faces and names of sorcerers carved into the wood.

Saggio touched the box's cover, as he looked at Jonah. He explained, "In this special box are the instructions for freeing a person from the spell that I just cast upon Fayrissa."

Saggio then slid the box toward Jonah. "Look inside the box, you'll see the exact incantation that I'll need to recite in order to reverse my spell."

Jonah opened the box. He saw a few sentences carved into the bottom of the box. He read the carved inscription.

South to West, we see the best.
As night is night, she must take flight.

"Jonah, I'll use those exact words to reverse my spell... but under one condition."

Jonah looked up and stared at Saggio.

Saggio took a piece of paper, tipped his writing quill into an inkwell, and began to write. When he finished, he slid the paper over to Jonah.

Jonah read from the paper as it rested on the desk.

- Sorcerer Apprentice Agreement -
I, Jonah Paladin, will work as Saggio's apprentice for three years. And in return Saggio will free Fayrissa from her spell immediately after James is captured and turned back into a creature.

When Jonah finished reading, Saggio leaned over and signed his name at the bottom of agreement. He then looked up and into Jonah's eyes. "Jonah, I hope that you will sign too. Together we will have untold powers and will gain unimaginable wealth. Nothing will stop us. I'll grant you some simple powers immediately after you sign. Then, as hard as Fayrissa may try, she will not be able to interfere when we two are united and working together."

Jonah was stunned. He stared at the paper, his mind was swirling. He had no real concept for what this would mean to him or what the risks would be. He was very fond of Fayrissa and had the deepest respect for her. And he knew that he owed her a huge debt for her help. But he was frightened to sign and hand over three years of his life to Saggio. Jonah thought, *"After three years as a sorcerer's apprentice, would it even be possible to return to a normal life? What would he have me do? How would this change me?"*

Saggio pressed him harder. "Jonah, I have a battle waging outside, and we need a decision from you very soon. But I will give you one half hour to decide, but no more time to sign this agreement after that."

Saggio turned over an hourglass, and as the sand began to slip through its narrow midpoint, he pointed to the half-hour marking on the hourglass. "Jonah, you have only one half hour to sign this agreement. After that time, there will be no other chance for you to sign and become my apprentice and partner... and Fayrissa will remain frozen indefinitely."

Saggio walked outside to watch the trees in the forest continue to transform into his relentless wooden army. He sat on the ground by his hut and smiled.

Jonah was frightened and confused. As he glanced over at Fayrissa's frozen and lifeless body, his heart raced and his chest and neck muscles tightened. He could feel and hear the blood thump inside his ears. Jonah wanted to see Fayrissa alive and free again, but the risks to his own life were high. He held his head with both hands as he struggled thinking about the three-year commitment to Saggio.

Finally, thirty minutes had passed. Jonah saw that the sand had passed the half-hour mark on the hourglass. His time was up.

Saggio walked into his hut, and sat down at the desk opposite Jonah.

"Jonah, we are out of time. What have you decided? Did you sign?"

Jonah looked nervous, and just stared.

"What's your decision, Jonah?"

Finally, Jonah slid both the wooden box and the agreement across the desk and over to Saggio.

Saggio began to smile as he quickly noticed that Jonah's signature was added to the paper. But then suddenly, Saggio's eyes squinted, and his head shook. Saggio's eyes quickly flashed up from the paper to Jonah.

"What is this Jonah? This is not the agreement I gave you. What did you do here? You wrote a different agreement? This is a different piece of paper. Are you joking?" Saggio pushed the paper across the desk and back over to Jonah.

Jonah hesitated. "Ummm… well, yes it's different. Saggio, I took a blank sheet of paper from your desk and wrote a new agreement for a one-year apprentice-ship. I signed it, and hope you will agree and sign too." Jonah read the new agreement.

- Sorcerer Apprentice Agreement -

I, Jonah Paladin, will work as Saggio's appren-tice for one year. And in return, Saggio will free Fayrissa from her frozen spell immediately af-ter James is captured and turned back into a creature. This agreement cancels and voids any other conversation or agreement for a three-year sorcerer apprenticeship.

Saggio looked furious. With a harsh voice, he told Jonah, "I cannot accept this! You should have signed my agreement when you had the chance." He frowned deeply. "You made the wrong choice Jonah, and time is up. You refused to sign, and so Fayrissa will remain frozen."

Jonah countered. "But Saggio, I will work for you as an apprentice for one year. And if you agree and sign too, we can both see Fayrissa alive and free again today."

"Jonah, this doesn't work, we wont be able to accomplish anything in one year. It will take me a year just to train you as a lesser sorcerer. Sorry, but I gave you one half hour to sign my agreement and you didn't. So, we have your decision. It's the wrong decision, and our Fayrissa will remain a statue."

Saggio grabbed the new agreement that Jonah drafted and held the paper in a candle's flame letting it burn. Its ashes dropped to the desktop in a pile.

Saggio abruptly stood up, pushing his chair backwards. "Jonah, your time is up, and we have no other business, it's time for you to leave."

But Jonah remained seated. He reached across the desk and tapped on the wooden box with just one finger.

Saggio gazed down at the box and then up at Jonah. He looked a little puzzled.

Saggio asked, "What about the box Jonah? I know what's in the box, we both do. And I will have no need for the inscription that's inside for a long time."

Jonah gently requested, "Please open it, and look inside."

Saggio stared hard at Jonah. His eyes drifted down to the box, and then up again at Jonah.

Jonah's eyes pleaded as he tapped on the box again. He nodded as he looked at Saggio, hoping he would open it.

Saggio stared and squinted at Jonah. Finally, he sat down again. He paused for a moment, but then his hand moved closer to the box. Slowly, he opened its cover. Then Saggio's eyes quickly fixed onto something inside the box. He reached inside the box, and lifted out a piece a paper. Immediately, Saggio erupted into loud peals of laughter.

Saggio laughed long and hard. Then he smiled at Jonah, and held up the paper he took from the box. It was Saggio's three-year apprentice agreement.

"So Jonah, you had signed my three-year agreement after all!"

Jonah nodded. "Yes, I signed it, and within one half hour as you required. But I hid the signed agreement in the box."

Saggio smiled and laughed. "So, let me understand Jonah. The one-year agreement that you drafted was a negotiation, an attempt to bargain for a better deal… one year instead of three. And you signed my agreement and hid it in the box while you tried to negotiate a one-year apprenticeship. Right?"

"Correct," Jonah replied. "And that's why my agreement also had wording that would cancel any other agreement for a three-year apprenticeship. I knew that I had signed *both* agreements, but if you signed my new one, it would cancel the three-year agreement."

"Brilliant! Fantastic!" Saggio laughed. "Jonah, you are truly a very smart young man indeed. What a terrific plan, very nice effort." Saggio paused then spoke softly. "But I'm sorry, Jonah, you lost this negotiation. However, believe me, you wont regret signing up for three years. And I can see that you'll make an excellent sorcerer's apprentice! We will be powerful and wealthy, I promise you."

Jonah said nothing. He looked across the room at Fayrissa's frozen body. She was still locked in the same position and still white as snow.

Jonah pointed at her and asked, "What about Fayrissa?"

"Why are you asking that Jonah? You know the answer. I'll free her after I capture James and turn him back into a creature. That's my part of our agreement. And I am not concerned about Faryissa after she is free. Her powers are not sufficient to give me much trouble, especially now that there are two of us. We will have complete control, power and great wealth."

Jonah was silent. He frowned.

"Jonah, I promise you that we will have an amazing three years. I realize this is a big commitment, thank you, and I will free Fayrissa soon enough, as promised. And I'm sure she will appreciate your sacrifice and devotion to set her free. She will be very grateful to you."

Jonah thought for a moment, and then asked, "What about you?"

"Me? What do you mean?" Saggio asked.

"Saggio, Fayrissa will be grateful for my sacrifice and devotion, but what's your sacrifice? Where's your devotion?"

Saggio looked at him sternly.

"Saggio, you're not freeing Fayrissa because of devotion. You're freeing her because we will have her overpowered by our united strength. It will be the two of us against her alone. You're showing your fear, not your affection."

"This is not about fear young lad. I don't need you Jonah. I can deal with Fayrissa without you, as I have for years already. I could free her at any time and deal with her interference if need be. But two of us will make things easier, that's all."

"That may be true Saggio, but how will all this change Fayrissa's opinion of you? Will she feel any closer to you as a result of our new agreement?" He paused. "Her opinion of you won't improve." Jonah chuckled. "Actually, she will dislike you even more. Her distance from you will be even greater after you win the battle, and she knows you pressured me into becoming your apprentice. She'll think your evil methods are growing. And that you will corrupt me too."

Saggio silently listened, as Jonah continued.

"If she is that important to you, Saggio, you need to take some risks to win her affection. Beating Fayrissa in this battle to recapture James in order to protect yourself wont get you any points with her. Instead Saggio, take a chance, and accept some risks now, or forever lose Fayrissa. That is the reality of where you are now. What will change for the better between you and her? Nothing! You are pushing the perfect woman for you farther and farther away."

Saggio glared at him. And while his gaze remained locked eye-to-eye with Jonah, Saggio was listening and thought deeply. Jonah was making sense.

"Now is the time to act Saggio. Release Fayrissa, give up the fight, and face up to these unknown consequences of the spell broken by James. Saggio, take the risk, show your courage, you know she's worth it. Is wealth and power really more important than love?

Haven't you lived alone, and without Fayrissa, for too long already? How many more years will you be without her? Maybe forever!"

Saggio looked away. He seemed to nod just a little with a blank look in his eyes.

The two sat silently.

A few moments passed.

Saggio looked uncomfortable and shook his head. Then a small smile appeared on his face. Unexpectedly, Saggio reached over the desktop, took the signed three-year agreement and held it up over the candle. Slowly, he lowered it into the flame. The words went up in smoke and ashes fell into a heap.

In a quiet voice Saggio spoke. "Jonah, you are right my friend. I've been stubborn and too occupied with my own successes. Each of my successes has pushed Fayrissa farther away from me, and winning the battle will make matters much worse. And she is worth more than the risks and these unknown consequences. It's time for a change."

Saggio stood again and faced Fayrissa. He saw a frozen beauty that needed life. Saggio took the wooden box and read the counter spell inscription on its bottom. Instantly, Fayrissa's eyelashes moved just a little. Soon she would be free. Saggio raced outside and signaled the retreat of his wooden army.

Then something mysterious happened. The wooden army lifted off the ground. Soldiers and horses floated past the forest treetops. Up high above, they turned into windmills, barns, wagons, fences and woodpiles that dropped down onto the town and the surrounding countryside.

In an instant, the people of Liguria regained their hope. They cheered from every corner of the town and throughout the countryside. All knew that the town and castle were now safe, and saved from the grips of destruction.

Deep in the forest a bright light shone. It lit the forest, the horizon and the sky. It was a sign... a sign that evil spirits no longer troubled the ancient forest.

Saggio lost the battle and met with the unknown consequences of the giant's good deed that broke his spell. The unknown swiftly became known... and Saggio's dark side was gone forever. The final consequence was that Saggio would be a force for good from this day forward. And Fayrissa learned how deeply Saggio really cared for her by his compassionate and selfless actions. And as time passed, the two would grow closer and closer.

CHAPTER 31
WELCOME.
NO ONE
EVIL INSIDE.

A FEW DAYS LATER in the forest, Fayrissa curiously watched Saggio repaint the sign that hung above his hut's front door. As he worked up on a ladder, Saggio's body blocked his work from Fayrissa's view, so she could not see the changes he was painting. He quickly finished repainting the sign, stepped down from his ladder and stood back to see his work.

"Look now Fayrissa," Saggio called to her.

At first, Fayrissa thought the sign looked unchanged and exactly the same as before. But she then looked more closely and saw one small change in the sign. Saggio's repainting of the sign had changed the punctuation. He simply moved a *period* over to the left of two words.

The sign had always read:
Welcome No One. Evil Inside.

After his repainting the sign read:
Welcome. No One Evil Inside.

"My, my, Saggio, you may not be evil any longer, but you're *still* a clever sorcerer, aren't you," she told him.

"A small circle can make a big difference," he answered, "and you, my Fayrissa, taught me the importance of circles." Saggio made a small circular motion with his paintbrush and then pointed it at the *period* he had just painted after the word *Welcome* on the sign.

The two held hands and went inside the hut. The door closed behind them. The glow of candlelight was flickering through a window until Saggio closed the curtains to keep Nico and Pico from peering inside the hut. The two squirrels felt snubbed and slighted when the curtains closed, but nevertheless they stayed stuck to the windowsill like a pair of furry barnacles.

Finally, the two little squirrels settled in for the night, and looked up at the twinkling stars while leaning against one another, until they were deep and fast asleep.

CHAPTER 32

DISCOVER THE EXTRAORDINARY

WEEKS LATER there was a grand celebration at the castle. The King invited all the people of Liguria. Beautiful music streamed from the forest's musical trees. Everyone danced... Jonah with Julia, Fayrissa with Saggio, King Leo with Queen Regina, and even Nico with Pico danced. Dr. Sano was invited as well, and danced with his wife while wearing his usual, unusual attire. But surprisingly, his wife's gown was impeccably fitted, she dressed like a queen and danced like an angel. And even Pico, who never spoke, was seen whispering gossip about the odd couple into

Nico's ear. The temptation was just too great for the little fellow.

This splendid celebration was the grandest of weddings. It was a wedding celebration for some very happy couples... the King's two sons and their brides, as well as Fayrissa and Saggio. Father Croce officiated the ceremony, and his little cat, Caesar, was seen peeking out from between his old black shoes. And after the wedding, there was also a special announcement that Julia and Jonah would marry next summer.

At this wonderful wedding and ball, everyone feasted on fresh warm breads, many fine pastas, roasts, fancy baked fish, fresh fruits, nuts and pastries, and drank the finest juices, ciders and wines. No festivity was ever more splendid. Fireworks lit the evening sky and cannons were blasted in celebration. The people of Liguria were never happier.

—⟨+⟩—

James gave Jonah and Julia the vineyard and round house as a wedding present, and as compensation for their captive work in the maze, as well as for guiding him to his most important good deed.

Jonah and Julia began working on the house, large windows and new rooms were being added. A central path was made through the vineyard maze to easily reach the house.

One section of the vineyard remained a maze. And local children were allowed to explore the maze, play, and pick grapes for their families. A sign hung over the entrance to the maze, it read:

Fiducia, Dura, Concordia

Nico and Pico were often found sitting on the sign and laughing as they ate nuts, and dropped their shells on anyone who passed under the sign. When the squirrels were there, no one entered the maze without having shells dropped on them, including King Leo and Queen Regina. Squirrels don't seem to care about royalty. You see, all humans look alike to squirrels... cousins or not.

One evening, Jonah and Julia were sitting near the maze and chatting away like a pair of parrots. As they watched Nico and Pico enjoy some nuts Jonah asked, "Julia, what ever happened to the feather you plucked from the sleeping giant? I gave my feather to the King, who keeps it locked away."

Julia got up went into the house and returned with a small white jar and a candle. She lit the candle and began to melt away the wax that sealed the lid onto the jar. She gently removed the lid and lifted the feather out.

"Here it is," she announced extending her hand holding the feather.

No sooner did she speak those words, a small breeze at their feet began to swirl leaves around in a circle. The breeze spun faster and faster and then grew wider until it swiftly swept the feather right from Julia's hand! Up and up it swirled above the vineyard maze. Higher and higher into the sky the feather drifted, then it traveled along a little ray of light that shined through a small opening in a cloud. They watched until the feather disappeared from sight.

Jonah and Julia looked at each other but said nothing, and both wondered... *How far will the feather travel? Where will it fall? Who will find it?*

A bird or some animal may find this feather and use it for building its nest. Or some person may pick it up and look it over for some ordinary use like decorating a hat, never realizing there may be an extraordinary use. As is often the case, most people fail to find that which is extraordinary in things that appear to be ordinary.

In similar ways, new ideas from ordinary sources often hold extraordinary solutions, but escape our attention. Often a small, ordinary thing that holds a ripe idea is dropped and lost, unnoticed for its unique importance. Hiding in the shadows of our thoughts, new solutions await a time for discovery. And inspiration springs from simple ideas... we need only to think and image.

And so, the next time you find a feather, or for that matter stumble across any ordinary looking thing or simple idea, think twice before discarding it too quickly. Look closely and you may discover that the ordinary may very well turn out to be extraordinary. Just like that feather plucked from a giant ...*a long, long time ago, deep in the forest of ancient Liguria.*

This Storyteller's Lament

As for me, the storyteller that I be,
I watched all, the weddings and fine ball,
They feasted full on foods so fine,
But gave me at this merry time,
Not even one half-glass of wine.

Finito

Fabula Scribo
Annum 1494
Liguria

EPILOGUE
GRANDPA'S UNCHARTED CHATS

I T WAS LATE, but my grandfather reached the end of this book about Jonah and his adventures. He silently stared at the author's poem on the last page.

But I interrupted his concentration. "Grandpa, is the author saying in his little poem, *This Storyteller's Lament,* that he was actually there at the weddings, and that the story in this book is true?"

"Jack, that's a good question," my grandfather replied as he closed the book. "But it's late and we're all pretty hungry. Let's have our discussion about this book's poem and story during dinner." Then Grandpa stood and said with a grin, "Let's get something to eat, and maybe have that half-glass of wine too."

"Maybe two half-glasses, right Grandpa?" I joked.

Grandpa nodded and smiled, and he put his arm across my shoulders as we walked to the taxi still parked outside.

We all hopped into the taxi and rode to a small but favorite restaurant in town for a late dinner. And I was certain that during tonight's meal, Grandpa without warning would hijack our conversation away from this book to another subject that strikes his fancy. But like a prickly grain of sand lodged in an oyster's shell from which a pearl is born, little pearls of wisdom often spring from Grandpa's uncharted chats.

And who knows, while Grandpa sips his glass of wine and chats, a small serendipitous story may surface that we'll all enjoy... and that is precisely the magic and marvel of storytelling. THE END

Storytelling Ideas for Young Children in Your Family

We hope you enjoyed reading *Extraordinary Thoughts of Jonah Paladin,* and found it to be both entertaining and educational. The story can be enjoyed by anyone regardless of age. This book can be read to children, a few chapters a night. It's been said that there is no better gift than reading a book with your children.

Also, there are sections of this book that can be told as individual short stories. These book sections are ideal for storytelling sessions with younger children in your family.

Readers are encouraged to improvise and embellish the story outlines below, and create their own versions for storytelling with the younger children in their families.

Storytelling Outline #1 for Young Children
Jonah Wins the King's Contests

A poor young lad named Jonah watched a King's contest that invited anyone to try and ride a very wild horse in the King's famous stable. Everyone that tried to ride this wild horse was bucked right off.

But by watching closely and thinking carefully, Jonah discovered that the horse was afraid of his own shadow. Jonah realized that fear of shadows is the reason why this horse bucked off every rider in the contest, and no one won. And Jonah thought that he could ride the horse and win the contest by riding at dusk when there are no shadows after the sun sets. So, he asked the King to ride this wild horse at dusk, and the King agreed.

The day for Jonah to ride in the contest finally came. Jonah mounted the wild horse, and the dim light of dusk cast no shadows on the ground. The horse stayed calm, and Jonah rode without the slightest trouble from the horse.

The crowd of spectators roared with applause, and the King awarded Jonah with the prize of gold coins. The King was so pleased and happy to see young Jonah win that he offered Jonah a second contest, as a way to win the wild horse too.

But when the King's stable master learned of the new contest, he became jealous of Jonah's success and also didn't want to give away the horse. So, he created a plan that would make Jonah lose this next contest. The stable master realized that Jonah won the last contest at dusk, and thought he can ruin Jonah's next ride by setting the contest time to Sunday morning. The stable master knew the bright morning light would cast shadows and frighten the horse. He hoped the frightened horse would then buck Jonah right off.

When Jonah learned that his next ride was on Sunday morning, he worried about riding the horse in the bright morning light. He knew the shadows would frighten the horse who would then kick and buck him off. So, Jonah went to his friend, Father Croce, for advice.

After Jonah explained his problem, Father Croce advised Jonah not to be so worried about the shadows. The priest told Jonah that the horse knows him now, because he rode the horse before. And he told Jonah, be confident and you will be able to ride and control this horse even if he sees shadows. But the priest also cautioned Jonah to hang on tightly, and stroke the horse's neck to calm the animal down. Father Croce also explained that talking to the horse will help keep the animal calm. The priest told Jonah to say, "Easy Now. Steady Now," while stroking the horse's neck. And if the horse bucks, he reminded Jonah to stay confident and believe in yourself.

Sunday morning came and Jonah was ready to ride in the contest. He mounted the horse, but the horse immediately saw its shadow in the bright morning light and became frightened. It kicked hard and almost bucked Jonah off. But Jonah held on tightly, stayed confident and followed Father Croce's instructions.

Finally, Jonah gained control of the horse, and finished the ride successfully. The crowd roared at Jonah's success, and the King happily gave the horse to Jonah. Jonah thanked the King and also Father Croce for his help and advice. Jonah rode his new horse home, and after he told his mother the story, she named the horse... Shadow!

Storytelling Outline #2 for Young Children
Julia Outsmarts a Cheating Giant and Wins Freedom

A girl named Julia was picking berries and became lost in the woods. A mysterious feathered giant, who lived deep in the woods, captured her.

The giant made Julia work in his vineyard maze. She tried to escape a few times, but got lost in the maze and could not find a way out.

A young lad named Jonah heard about Julia and tried to rescue her. But he too became lost in the maze, and the giant captured him as well.

After a few days, the giant finally offered a chance for their freedom and suggested they play a game. He put two grapes in a bag. The giant told Jonah and Julia, if they picked the round grape from the bag they would be free to go. But if they picked out a squashed grape, they must stay working longer in the vineyard, and not try to escape anymore.

But the giant cheated and put *two squashed grapes* in the bag! So, there was no way to pick a round grape and win. Julia realized the giant was cheating. But she had an idea, so she reached into the bag to pick out one of the squashed grapes. As she lifted the grape out of the bag, she suddenly sneezed, and she dropped the grape on the ground. The grape she picked was now lost among many other round and squashed grapes on the ground.

Julia told the giant that she dropped and lost the grape that she had picked out, and doesn't know if it was a round or squashed grape. But then she told the giant that by looking at which grape *remains in the bag*, we would know which grape was picked out and dropped.

She then picked out the other squashed grape from the bag. She showed it to the giant, and announced that she must have picked out and dropped the *round grape*.

The giant realized he was outsmarted by clever Julia, and reluctantly freed his two prisoners.

Storytelling Outline #3 for Young Children
An Evil Sorcerer Cast a Spell and Turned a Prince into a Feathered Giant

An evil sorcerer cast a spell on the King's son, which turned him into a feathered giant. The giant ran deep into an ancient forest to hide his monstrous appearance from everyone.

The next day when the King could not find his son, he became saddened and very sick as he missed his lost son. No one could cure the King, and he felt worse every day. But a strange doctor visited the sick King and explained that a feather from a feathered giant can restore the King's health.

The giant lived in a small house past the ancient forest, and his house was surrounded by a vineyard maze to keep people away. And because the evil sorcerer lived in the forest, no one could easily travel through the forest to even get close to the giant's vineyard and house.

Yet, a brave lad named Jonah wanted to get a feather and help the sick King. So, he climbed across the forest's treetops, high above the sorcerer's hut, so he would not be seen. By climbing this way, Jonah safely reached the giant's vineyard maze.

The lad explored the vineyard maze being careful not to get lost in it, and looked for a feather that may have fallen off the giant. Jonah soon found a feather in the maze, and quietly climbed back to town by traveling across the treetops, and right over the evil sorcerer's hut again.

When Jonah returned to the King's castle, the feather cured the King's sickness, and also broke the evil spell, which then turned the feathered giant back into the King's son. When the King saw his son again, he hugged him tightly. Afterwards, the son explained that he ran away into the forest to hide his monstrous appearance from everyone.

The broken spell also turned the evil sorcerer into a good sorcerer. So, the sorcerer wanted to repaint and change an old sign on his hut that welcomed no one.

When the sorcerer repainted the hut's sign, he only changed the punctuation on the sign. He simply moved a *period* over to the left of some words, and entirely changed the sign's meaning.

The sign had always read:
Welcome No One. Evil Inside.

After his repainting the sign read:
Welcome. No One Evil Inside.